THE SKY-HIGH WITNESS

Sarah Ickes

Originally Published October 2025

Historical Mystery | Action and Adventure | Clean Story

Martin turned around to see the blur
of Margaret dashing back to where her
father was still chatting with Kathleen in
the lobby, and shook his head in jest.

"That would be Miss Everton, who was a
witness to the bank robbery earlier today.
Her father, Thomas, also has a statement
to make."

THANK YOU...

to my Beta Reader, Sherry, for taking time out
to help me make this book the best it can be.

A SPECIAL NOTE...

Many of the references to the historical objects and events in this book, have real research to back them up. If you are interested in taking a peek behind the writer's curtain, to glimpse into the works I used for inspiration, you can check out three bullet points included in the back of this novel, as well as visit my website for a more indepth look.

www.SarahIckesArt.com

Some words in this novel are older, and are not spelling errors. Definitions can be found at my website.

Thank you for trying out my story. And I hope that you enjoy the trip into a time when the world was just as crazy as it is today.

and don't miss out on all the action!

<u>Murial Robertson Mysteries</u>
The Serpent's Star
Angled for Revenge
A Counterfeit of Death
An Ancient Poison (coming soon)

<u>Vectra Tillerman Adventures</u>
Written Wings
The Fall of Time (coming soon)

<u>Vectra and Murial Cross-Over</u>
The Nation's Grief (coming soon)

<u>A Family's Masterpiece Series</u>
A Family's Masterpiece (coming soon)

<u>Cybil Lawson Mysteries</u>
The Ghost of Christmas Pastel
In Plein Air Sight (coming soon)

As Always, For G.

To Rev. Joseph A. Murray D.D. and Rev. Thorn,

Whose contributions to preserving the historical accounts of Carlisle, made my research ever more achievable, and that much more interesting! You may no longer dwell in this life, but you are not forgotten.

And to Chris M.,

Whose support of my writing is not taken for granted.

CHARACTERS

Margaret Everton	Eleven-Year-Old Young Lady
Thomas Everton	Margaret's Father, General Store Owner
Nancy Everton	Margaret's Mother, Runs the General Store with Thomas
Coon	Friend of the Evertons, Used to Work for the Stagecoach
Kathleen McKnee	Nancy's Childhood Friend
Martin McKnee	Kathleen's Husband, Owns A Company That Makes Safes
John Wise	Aeronaut
Reverend Thorn	Local Reverend
Rebecca	Little Girl at the Ascension
Bobby	Little Errand Boy
Mr. Arnold	Bank Manager
Wilfred	Bank Teller
Bank Teller	Wilfred's Co-Worker
Gerome Wellington	Law Student
James Guthrie	Silversmith and Clockmaker

CHARACTERS

Gene Moore	Hotel Manager
Mr. Adler	Hotel Employee
Frederick	Hotel Employee
Charles Thurber	Hotel Guest

The Sheriff	The Sheriff
Ace Highsmith	Candidate for Sheriff
Donald Sutherby	Candidate for Sheriff

And of course, the bad guys...

CHAPTER 1

Margaret Everton looked disappointed at the sky far above the window in her bedroom. Today was the day she had been looking forward to, ever since she saw the advertisement in the May 10th issue of the *Carlisle Herald*. The same issue, in point of fact, that unexpectedly sealed her fate come the first of September. How could she forget that cringeworthy date of doom for which she would dreadedly leave, all that she knew, in order to travel southeast toward the town of Chambersburg. According to the Seminary and Boarding School for Young Ladies, their area was touted as being "one of the healthiest in the country." However, Margaret was not convinced that their quality of air heavily differed from that of Meyer's Bend.

Despite her constant refusals to go, and Margaret's insistence that her help was invaluable to her parents' general store, the decision had been made. Her mother already sent word to the school earlier in the week, and there was nothing Margaret could do about it. While the idea of traveling to an unknown place sparked her curiosity with intrigue, she could not keep the fear of leaving their small village out of her mind. *I will not be able to conduct any new experi-*

ments while I am away either.

Margaret's thoughts soon began to wander as she stared into the angry weather. When her father knocked on the door to her room, however, she snapped back to the present as he waited a heartbeat for her to respond. "Hey Teacher, you up already?"

"Unfortunately." His daughter's brown hair bounced against her rounded face as she plopped upon her bed in the blue dress she planned to wear. 'Teacher' had been her nickname since her first spoken word at eleven months old: book. Given that her mother was an avid reader, and custodian over the two-shelved library housed within their store, the word was in her blood. In the prior two years, she had read more books than everyone in their village had over three decades; so it was only natural that she wanted to become a school teacher. But for now, all she wished for were the clouds to dissipate and the storms to head north. "This weather sure has been upset as of late."

Mr. Everton observed the bags under his daughter's eyes from the sleepless night she'd just endured; kept awake by the loud peals of thunder and brilliant flashes of lightening from dusk to dawn. He gathered by the way her hands refused to be still, that Margaret feared the worse for the day's festivities. Though they were to be held later in the afternoon, the current outlook was not promising.

Margaret suddenly turned around to see her father coming over to sit beside her on the bed. "Do you think they will defer the ascension?"

"Perhaps. However, the sun has barely risen above the horizon, and his flight is not scheduled until two o'clock. That leaves plenty of time for the weather to clear before he is to lift off from the square." Lightly tapping his rough index finger on the tip of his daughter's nose, Mr. Everton was able to crack her weary face into the pleasant smile he knew and loved. "Who knows? Maybe even *you* will be able to teach Mr. Wise something new today."

"I highly doubt I could tell Mr. Wise anything he does not already know about aerial travel. He has flown far into the sky thirty-nine times, and I've merely lifted ten feet above the ground in my own experiments." Margaret's smile quickly faded back into disappointment while her father rolled his eyes.

"You say that as if everyone has accomplished that much in their own lives as a daily chore, rather than the achievement it truly is." His hands messed up her hair in a playful manner, attempting to brighter her mood. But Margaret hastily moved out of his reach and asked for him to stop ruining her perfect curls. "I apologize, My Lady. Did not realize you were so careful as to your appearance, all of a sudden."

Her father had grown accustomed to his daughter's normally dirty hands, face, and feet, she'd obtain from tinkering on her flying machine. As her hair was often frizzy from the summer's humidity, and frozen solid in the winter's arctic cold, he often joked that she looked more like a wild animal than a civilized girl of the 1840s. His wife had even once threatened to remove the machine if their daughter did not keep herself looking more presentable; to which, Margaret retaliated by sleeping in the barn with the other "animals" like her. Of course, according to his wife, their daughter's stubborn attitude came from his side of the family.

"I just want to look my best for when we go into Carlisle. That's all. It is not every day, or every month even, that we get to venture somewhere else." Margaret's fingers instinctively went for the top of her head to inspect the damage that had been done. "You would not wish for me to appear shameful, now would you?

"No. No. We certainly would not want that to happen." He chuckled half to himself, and half to the air, as he saw her trying to act years older than her true age. "I am sure the local newspapers will be in attendance, and looking for public commentary to publish. One must look her best, in case she were to be asked."

Margaret stuck her tongue out at her father, just as her mother's voice could be heard at the door. They both turned to find her peering inside to the see them sitting by the window, and she sighed with exasperation. "There you are. After I searched all over for you, only to find that you are hiding from Coon in Margaret's room."

"He saw me?"

Mrs. Everton's head slowly nodded. "I swear that man has been sitting outside our store for longer than a moon cycle. He was asking about that…"

"Order I placed for him last week?" Her husband's head swung from side to side. "I told him that the bullets would not arrive until the first week of June at the earliest. The ones he purchased are coming down from Boston."

"Well, I realize that, Thomas. But you know how worried he becomes until those boxes are sitting in his hands. Especially after he received a new gun from…that company he likes…Thurber and Allen." Margaret's mother gave her classic stern look that promptly suggested he head downstairs to tend to the matter himself. It was the same glare she used on Mr. and Mrs. Brown's children whenever they tried sneaking a few jelly beans from the glass candy jars, and Margaret hoped to use it as the perfect weapon against her future students.

"Alright. I shall go and have a chat with him. Why he is up at this hour, I have no idea." Thomas stood up from his daughter's bed, passing his wife as she walked in to make sure Margaret had everything she needed for the day's trip ahead.

"Yes, Mother. All is packed in my bag and ready to go!" Margaret sometimes felt as though her mother would never treat her like the mature eleven-year-old that she was, and crossed her arms in front of her chest out of frustration. "You need not be concerned with me any longer." *Having enrolled me in a boarding school, against my will, is proof enough of that. Apparently my usefulness around here is no longer required.*

"Don't you take that tone of voice with me, Margaret Anne Everton! You are acting more like a child this past week, than I think you ever have before."

Margaret was not about to surrender her stance. "If you would just come to Carlisle with us, to see Mr. Wise take to the air in his marvelous balloon, then you could see why aerial flight is so fascinating to me, and…" She instantly silenced her words at the sight of her mother's raised hand for quiet.

"Someone has to stay behind to manage this place. Besides, no balloon trip is going to change my mind about you attending that boarding school in the fall."

"But Mother, who will look after my flying machine while I am gone? And without it, how can I run anymore experiments?"

"It will be safe in the barn. We can even have Coon check in on it from time to time."

"I suppose…" Margaret's lips pouted like a hungry puppy, feeling the weight of a losing battle resting solely on her shoulders. She had wondered if her wealthy friend could have his staff watch over it for her, but the thought of imposing on him like that, caused her to hesitate. Even when her mother blocked the window by standing in front of it, she barely acknowledged her with a slight tilt of her head.

"Margaret, why do you see me as the bad one in this? Hmm? The school has better facilities than our local one. You will be able to ask questions of all sorts, read more science books than you can imagine, and obtain a strong footing to becoming the teacher you have always wanted to be."

"You sound like their advertisement in the paper." Margaret kept her mouth mute on the fact that she had overheard her parents talking about the school's cost roughly three nights ago. After they decided on how much more money was needed to save each week, she feared they'd be reduced to eating bread and water for nearly every meal. But like always, her mother had a keen intuition that could tell when Margaret was hiding something behind those inquisitive eyes of hers, and Mrs. Everton squatted down to be at her level.

"We are going to be fine, Margaret. Honest. I know it's scary to be in a new place without either of us, and in an area that is unlike Meyer's Bend. However, that just means that it is an adventure, waiting to be explored. You will get to meet other girls from different cities while school is in session, and come home during breaks. We are only a train ride away; so it is not as though you are traveling across the Atlantic Ocean."

Regardless of her daughter's unchanged mood, Mrs. Everton was seemingly satisfied with her talk, and popped upright quicker than a prairie dog. "Now then, September is too distant in the future to be worrying about. Today is May 27th, and you have a balloon ascension to attend."

"NANCY!" Thomas hollered from the first floor where their store resided, trying to keep Coon from sitting down on an old chair beside the vegetables. "Mrs. Ishmailer needs some bolts of fabric you were supposed to handle!"

Margaret saw her mother's eyes widened in alarm. "Oh my, heavens! I completely forgot that her daughter is due to come home tomorrow…and…and I was supposed to deliver her order on Thursday!" Mrs. Everton quickly dashed to the door to amend her mistake, leaving Margaret alone in her room once again.

About five minutes later, as the sky was finally beginning to lighten, her father called up the stairs. "Since we are all up, we might as well get a head start. Your chariot awaits, Teacher!"

Margaret found it rather difficult to contain her excitement. She had only visited the bustling town of Carlisle three times before, and each one rewarded her with a chocolate bar from the shop on High Street. Her father, on the other hand, saw this occasion as the perfect business opportunity, after hearing the rumors that everyone was to be present. Yes, Sir. The whole town had arranged a jolly celebration to see Johnathan Wise's fortieth ascension from the Town's Square. Even the postal worker told them a band had been hired, according to the man's cousin who had a trumpet-playing friend. *Today is going to be the best day ever!*

"Coming!" Margaret raced to the first floor with a bag in hand, and followed him out the back door with a larger-than-life smile spread on her face. *No matter what happens, I am going to enjoy every minute of this trip!*

CHAPTER 2

Thomas Everton drove his horses past Dickinson College, and alongside the train tracks leading them toward the heart of Carlisle. Margaret's eyes refused to blink for several minutes, as she studied the people coming in from all over the county. The closer their cart came within sight of the brick buildings on High Street, the larger the crowd seemed to be growing. All across the sidewalks, folks chatted with one another, and entered shops with sale signs advertised in their windows. Complete strangers were disembarking from the yellow passenger train cars that had recently arrived from Shippensburg, and they also found easy conversations with those passing by. It was a far different scene than the quiet countryside Margaret knew, and she could instantly feel her senses being overwhelmed by all of the commotion.

"Do you happen to remember what Mrs. McKnee looks like?" Thomas asked his preoccupied daughter. "She has not visited your mother in so long, that I could easily miss her amongst these hundreds of people."

"Huh?" Margaret had barely heard a word he said, but was rather fixated on the centre square just ahead of them.

From what she could see, the large intersection contained four decently-sized green spaces that were lined with roped fences. Two churches had been built on the grassy fields to the northern side of High Street, while the court-house and market-house sat on the southern side. In Margaret's opinion, the townscape appeared well-gridded underneath the clumps of spectating Pennsylvanians, who were starting to consume the entire town.

Horses carried stragglers attempting to cut through heavily-trafficked sections, as others began to shout at carts with owners slow to move toward the inundated stables. Closer to where a few banners had been hung in the trees, band members were rushing to their designated seats after grabbing some last minute food from a stand across the street. And further back, barely visible to Margaret's unaided eye, stood a commanding presence by a group of military soldiers from the local barracks. Their mounted artillery had certainly captivated a number of people's attentions, including the younger kids who gathered in front of the cannons.

"Margaret? Margaret, are you listening to me?"

"What?" Finally turning her head to see her father with an exasperated look on his face, Margaret apologized for her absentmindedness. "I'm sorry, Father. This place…. there is simply too much to look at, and I was trying to see the balloon…the Aerial…that should be in the centre square. But I do not believe it has been inflated yet."

"Good. Because I need you to help me first. We are supposed to meet up with Mrs. McKnee at the Mansion House Hotel, so she can watch you as I talk with a few men about business prospects. Do you recall what road your mother said it would be on?"

Margaret took a moment to think before she answered

his question. "I think she said it is at the corner of High Street and Pitt Street. Oh, and the train tracks lead right to the front door. So it was back there." Her hand pointed behind their cart and down the way they just came.

"Perfect!" Mr. Everton's head shook from side to side at the idea of turning around in the congested area. While his face did beam with pride at his daughter's sharp memory, which apparently came from his wife's side of the family, he sincerely wished she had spoken up much sooner than she had. "Once we get turned around, it should be no more than a few minutes before we are there!"

"Do you think we could stop at the chocolate shop before we leave for home later today?" Margaret excitedly asked. She could already taste the chocolate melting in her mouth, and wondered what made it so smooth on the tongue.

"We will have to see his hours. Many of the shops keep shortened days on Saturday." Thomas cautioned. He proceeded to pull on the reins and skillfully navigated his way to the hotel by coming in on Pitt Street. "At least we arrived safe and sound."

Margaret glanced up at the multi-storied building that had once been visited by Dr. Benjamin Rush himself in 1784; which was a site to behold as the train's whistle disrupted the normal chatter along the sidewalks. But the beautiful woman standing at the entranceway could not have gotten lost in the midst of the wandering crowd. Her non-moving brown hair was pinned toward the back of her head, while her blue eyes searched the incoming traffic for any sign of her friend's family. As soon as she spotted their cart nearing the sidewalk, a charming smile spread across her sparsely-wrinkled face.

"Thomas! Over here!" She waved her gloved hand in

a restrained manner, and calmly approached to greet the little girl who had grown so much in the past few years. "My goodness! This could not be Margaret Everton, I see here before me! Why, she looks to be almost sixteen by now." A short wink from the middle-aged woman helped to remove any nerves Margaret had at seeing her mother's childhood friend again.

"Hi, Kathleen! Been too long since we last saw you in Meyer's Bend." Mr. Everton elbowed his daughter to climb down from the bench seat as he talked to Mrs. McKnee. "Nancy wanted me to pass along her thanks for you agreeing to take Margaret to the ascension today."

"Not at all. I am still ever grateful to her for helping my dear aunt through her…illness." Kathleen's cheeks turned slightly pink as she thought back to the awful bout of tuberculosis that took her aunt's life nearly four years ago. "Nancy is simply an angel with the sick. I told her that she was wasting her talent for nursing in that general store of yours. But I quite think she is happier there than I ever did see her."

"Well, she certainly does a fine job with running everything in an orderly fashion." Thomas then asked her about the nearby stables for their horses Josephine and Abraham. After Mrs. McKnee told him that the ostler had recently taken down another traveler's horse for a drink of water, he went in search of the man to sort out the fees while a hotel staff member tended to the cart.

After Margaret's father left her with his wife's friend, Kathleen took the opportunity to show her around the Mansion House Hotel; a place that had been recently furnished through the use of advertisements in the local newspapers. "This place houses two parlor rooms, an eating room for sixty people, and sixteen bedrooms! Now, it is a far cry from the grand ones in Philadelphia and New York

City, but it is quite a luxury here."

"It certainly is bigger than any building I have ever been inside before."

Mrs. McKnee led Margaret up to the top floor, telling her about their stay as they took the stairs before making a right turn. "My husband is friends with Willis Foulk, who is leasing this building. So our rate is rather low in comparison to others. Though, do not tell anyone else this, but I would gladly pay the full price. The rooms are adequately adorned and our view looks toward the centre of town. My husband asked for me to show you what we are able to see from here. I told him it was foolish to think that you would prefer a glance from faraway, then that of being up close to the balloon in person. Alas, he does not have an interest in such matters as you do. His affairs lie solely in the world of safes and lock boxes."

As Kathleen opened the door to her room, Margaret eagerly raced to the window in order to peer through the glass. Her eyes searched the landscape with great anticipation at seeing the balloon being inflated with gas, but she quickly withdrew from the glass pane out of sheer disappointment. "The trees obscure my view far too much."

"Would you like to be closer?" Mrs. McKnee happily offered, with a caring twinkle in her stare.

"If it would not be a bother to you…" The last thing Margaret wanted to be was an imposition on her kind hostess.

"No trouble at all. Of course we can." The smile on her face washed away any fear that Margaret had about asking. "I just need to grab my pardessus and switch my bonnet for something more suitable to the occasion." She darted into a closet to grab the items, and took a look in the mirror to ensure her appearance was otherwise still intact. "I have

Martin waiting to escort us, down in the bar. Based on what Nancy has told me about your experiments, I believe that you are going to be a great teacher someday. Maybe, even in the field of science?"

Margaret suddenly felt more at ease with her mother's friend. Mrs. Everton had constantly reminded her daughter that not everyone in the world was as kind as those living in their hometown, and that she should keep her mind sharp at all times. *Observation is the most important key to survival,* was the saying that had been carved into Margaret's brain since she could remember. "Mrs. McKnee, do you miss living in Meyer's Bend?"

"I did in the beginning; and still do now and again. However, I must insist that you call me Kathleen. You were but a foot long when I first saw you, so it seems wrong that you continue to use formalities." She bore an even larger smile that would have warmed the coldest of human hearts. "Are you ready?"

"Ready as I will ever be." Margaret straightened out her skirt and grabbed onto Kathleen's hand as they returned to the staircases.

"Once we reach the lobby, I will have to send word to Martin that he is to meet us outside of the bar. Due to the number of people coming and going, I must insist that you stay beside me, you hear? It is my job to keep you out of trouble, and that is just what I intend on doing."

"Only if you can keep up." Margaret playfully moved faster near the bottom of the stairs, and suddenly bumped into a man walking toward the bar from the check-in counter. "Oh, I'm terribly sorry, Sir."

"That's quite alright, Miss. Have fun in life while you still can, that's always been my mantra." His semi-gruff hands patted her on the shoulder as he gave a formal nod to Mrs. McKnee. He then shot young Margaret a crooked grin between his thick mustache and beard, before continuing on his way. Though his palms had noticeably been through tough labor, his hands were far too clean to be that of a rancher, and his clothes were too large for his build.

"Ah, Frederick. Would you please tell my husband that we will be requiring his services?" Kathleen instructed the hotel worker, who gave her a silent nod in turn. Following him into the bar with her eyes, Margaret gazed into the room where she was not welcomed, and saw another man standing by himself in a small corner. He lit the cigar protruding from his lips, appearing to be waiting for the one she bumped into at the foot of the stairs. While his taller frame was more intimidating than the other, there was no mistaking their facial resemblances when they stood side by side. Remembering what Coon had told her from his earlier days of working for the stagecoach, she studied them until Kathleen poked her in the ribs.

"Come on, Margaret. What men do in their own time is their business alone." Glancing up to see Thomas coming up to the front door, Kathleen swiftly made her way over to him, and asked how things went at the stables.

"The ostler was nowhere to be found. I tried to pay the boy who was handling the horses there instead, and he informed me that his father solely dealt with the money. Apparently he is trying to locate a Mr. Thurber in the bar?" He thanked his daughter for pointing toward the room where the two men were chatting, and cleared up his business just as Frederick came back from delivering his message.

"Mr. McKnee says that he will join you in about five minutes." The worker reported to Kathleen, who tipped him a few cents for the effort.

"Wait, Martin was in there? How did I manage to miss him?" Thomas wondered aloud. "Where are you ladies going, in point of fact?"

"We're headed to the square to watch the balloon flight!" Margaret's eyes widened like a kitten as she pleaded with him to allow her to attend. "Kathleen said that Martin was waiting to take us."

Her father looked over at Mrs. McKnee with uncertainty painted on his face. "Do you not have to pay to go inside the arena? I thought one of the windows in this building would provide a nice view."

Kathleen waved his worry off like a mildly annoying fly. "My treat. The admission fee is worth every cent so she can witness this spectacle from the ground level."

"Then at least permit me the honor of escorting you two there. I happen to have business with James Guthrie on the other side of the square, and I hope to catch him at his shop on Harper's Row before he closes for the day."

"I would be delighted! Frederick, please inform my husband that he is off duty this afternoon, which will most likely please him, and tell him that Mr. Everton will be taking us to the square instead." Kathleen gave him a few more coins before they went to exit the busy building. "Martin hates crowds so much so, that I am willing to bet he'll consider you to be a brother from this day onward, Thomas."

"That is hardly necessary, as I consider this a privilege. However, I would call us even, if he has any good connections to chocolate shops. I know someone who has a fondness for sweet desserts." Mr. Everton winked at his daughter as the trio left the emptying hotel, and walked down High Street to join in the festivities.

CHAPTER 3

Bells could be heard all around town, as the clock atop the court-house chimed at noon. It was time for the balloon to finally be inflated with gas, and everyone lined around the ropes to see how it was done. Margaret struggled to suppress the urge to charge into the growing crowd and leave Kathleen behind with her father. It was difficult for her to contain what felt like a dream come true; to finally see the man in person she had read newspaper articles about, and heard stories told by the wealthiest member of Meyer's Bend.

While her father only had the local papers delivered to their store on a regular basis, one of their "neighbors" was a high-profiled business owner; who maintained a seasonal estate near her hometown. Whenever he spent a few days away from the city's faster pace of life, Margaret would pick his brain with all sorts of questions. He brought back various newspapers for her to read, and would delight her with tales of new inventions his friends were investing in. She never worried if her presence annoyed the older gentleman, as her mother had often cautioned; since his weary face enlightened at seeing her bright smile. In a way, his words had been a doorway for her imagination, and she found herself wishing he was there to join in on the excitement of it all.

"Margaret, the ladies' section is over there." Kathleen bumped her in the shoulder, bringing the girl's mind down from the clouds above. Mrs. McKnee then led her over to the designated area, and turned to wave good-bye to Mr. Everton. "We will be alright. You should go and talk with Mr. Guthrie while you can."

"Will do. I'll catch up with you two later!" Thomas called out, finding the dense crowd to be slightly suffocating as he scouted out the few openings. "Have fun, Margaret!" His face quickly faded into the waves of people descending upon the square as he made his way across the large intersection, in search of Harper's Row.

How could he think of talking about watches at a time like this? Margaret shook her head out of disbelief. *What could be much more fascinating than seeing man fly in the air?* She thought back to the conversation her father had with Coon earlier that same week. They discussed the watch and silversmith shop, after a local farmer had recommended him, and she wondered if he was picking up an order for one of their customers. *Mother's birthday is in June, though. So perhaps he is looking into a present for her instead?*

With Margaret's thoughts on everything else, except where she was headed, her feet almost stepped atop a man's blackened shoes, until Kathleen pulled her out of the potential collision. "Reverend Thorn," Mrs. McKnee's abrupt voice caught the girl by surprise, "it is so good to see you. How is Susan? I missed our date for lunch this past Tuesday, and forgot to send a message about rescheduling."

"She is doing fine, thank you. In fact, she is working

on having some of the hymnals rebounded as we speak." He smiled with a sense of humor in his cheeks, and talked about their church's forthcoming picnic for the following afternoon. As they chatted over the food each person was to bring, Margaret could feel her frustrations mounting on the inside. Not only did she already fail at staying observant of her surroundings, but she desperately wanted to reach a better viewing spot as soon as possible. "Yes, Ma'am. Susan said that my duty was to get God's word ready for tomorrow. But I could not miss something as grand as this balloon flight, and even God rested one day for the good of our humanly health."

"Indeed, Reverend." Kathleen introduced Margaret to the gentleman, and explained her unique interest in Mr. Wise's work.

"Why, I admire your inquisitive nature, young lady, and you have the most fortuitous timing, I do say. Mr. Wise, and myself, were just discussing that very same thing a moment ago." He beamed with a genuine happiness in his eyes, and tapped the ground with his right foot. "Besides our shared first name, we realized our mutual fascination with aerial navigation. Though, I must admit, that his visions encompass a far greater worldly reach than I ever imagined."

Suddenly, Margaret's face widened with intrigue. "You mean, you *actually* spoke with Mr. Wise?"

"I most certainly did. Elsewise, that would be lying; which is a double sin for a man of the cloth." Reverend Thorn pulled out a few pieces of paper, along with a pencil, from the pocket of his outer jacket. The first side of the folded pages appeared to have disjointed notes cluttering its otherwise blank surface. "Truthfully, I am going to document this special day for the town with a time line of events, which I hope to publish in the *Carlisle Herald*."

"That's wonderful, Reverend. But, what is Mr. Wise like?" Margaret hastily asked.

"He is a scientific mind like I have never met before, Miss Everton. One who dares to dream with the gift of eloquent words such as that of Miguel de Cervantes. Though I dare not say that loudly, for fear of being mugged by his devoted readers." He took a pause to cough after a bug landed in his mouth, before continuing onward. "Mr. Wise told me about his recent trip to Philadelphia, in search of financial aid to pay for his way across the Atlantic Ocean in a balloon. As he described it, they were highly interested until they saw how serious he truly was in making balloons the new mode of transportation. This exhibit today is part of his campaign for drawing attention to those *very* same plans. In fact, he mentioned something about seeing an inventor he recognized from Philadelphia, being amongst the crowd here today."

"It is a marvelous notion, is it not? To fly from America to London under wind power would be revolutionary!" Margaret remembered that the ad in the paper had mentioned Mr. Wise bringing a smaller balloon with him, in case he decided to make his ascension a royal trip to England itself. It was the same intrepid idea that Balloonist Charles Green had also been striving for in Europe, without much success.

"Oh yes! I, for one, can see a religious advantage to such a splendid way of traveling. Could you not see a minister preaching from the heavens to his flock below? Spreading the everlasting gospel like an angel to the souls who dwell upon this earth?"

Margaret merely returned a quiet smile, unsure of what to say about the Reverend's dream. *At a certain altitude, I do not believe anyone would be able to hear his sermons.*

Though, I do not wish to dampen his sense of optimism.

"That would be a grand thing indeed, Reverend." Kathleen wished him well on his report of the day's festivities, and then hastily ushered Margaret toward the other women awaiting in their area. "The Reverend is a little eccentric; but he means well, and is a very kind soul. His wife, Susan, happens to be the daughter of the Honorable Judge Hamilton." She leaned closer to the young girl's ear, in order to whisper her next remarks. "Personally, I believe that her lineage helps immensely in their social standings."

At this point, Margaret was done with talking. She was not there to chat with others about the town's social gossip, nor the controversy of using the court-house's bell for a purpose other than religious, legal, or emergency means. And she did not venture away from home to watch the event through adults' arms and legs either. Mr. Wise's balloon was over a quarter of the way inflated by now, and Margaret was determined to observe the process at the front of the section.

Squeezing between two women dressed in plaid, standing at the ropes, she left Kathleen behind three rows back, and suddenly found herself beside a seven-year-old girl. Her eyes scanned the area where the "Aerial" was slowly rising into the air, in the hopes that she could see Mr. Wise supervising the process. "I don't see him. Where is Mr. Wise?" Margaret muttered the questions under her breath.

"He be talking with his son and wife over there." The little girl pointed to a spot located at the opposite corner of the grassy patch. She then readjusted how she held her younger sister's doll with her right arm, before continuing to speak in her higher-pitched voice. "I saw him talking with our minister just before, too."

Margaret figured that the black-haired girl had meant

Reverend Thorn, and decided not to say anything more than a quick "thank-you" in turn. She had no interest in getting dragged into another long discussion about unimportant matters happening in town. About an hour later, however, she hesitantly reached into the pocket of her dress, in search for the last piece of candy she stowed for the trip. And just as she went to pull it out, a dark shadow fell right upon her face. Curiously, Margaret looked up at the taller man from the bar, blocking the sun with the large frame of his body, as he appeared to be searching the crowd for someone in particular.

Though she could not see all of his face in the hotel, she took note of the black patch covering his right eye; now visible as he swiftly moved away in the direction of the courthouse. Margaret continued to watch where the suspicious man was headed, observing a blurred figure joining him on the steps to the justice building. *How odd. What is the real reason for those two to be here?* In Margaret's humble opinion, something was not right.

"He's the mean one." The little girl abruptly stated, a little too loud for her mother's likeness.

"Rebecca! I am having a conversation. Please keep your voice down." She mindlessly tapped her child on the arm, before resuming her discussion with a blonde-haired seamstress.

"Wait, you know that man?" Margaret asked the little girl as she pointed toward the man's back, trying to keep a lookout in case he glanced over his shoulder at them.

"Yes. He is the pirate who is in search of treasure." Rebecca whispered with a sparkle in her eyes. She motioned for Margaret to come closer, so her mother would not correct her again. "I first saw him talking near the water pump by the Market-House. He told his friend that 'chickens were better than pigs for the bounty they wanted.' Then, he walked back down the street with a limp, and that eyepatch on his face…exactly like a pirate! He even said he was one when I asked him."

A limp? Margaret took another gander over where the man had recently disappeared into the crowd. *He walked with no issues a moment ago.* "Maybe he was carrying something heavy?"

"No idea. But I thought his hand was hurt earlier, for he kept it in his pocket."

Margaret had not realized she'd spoken her last question aloud, and gave Rebecca a smile for not interrupting her ramblings. "Well, if you have no clue, than neither do I."

The little girl soon opened her mouth again, with a flash of eagerness in her gaze, and was about to say something else, when another shadow quickly fell upon them. Margaret could barely keep her mouth closed as she glanced up to see Mr. Wise, himself, standing right in front of her!

CHAPTER 4

While John Wise's words seemed to address all of the women waiting for the ascension to take place, Margaret swore he looked directly at her as he spoke. "Ladies, surely this is too far away in order to witness such a marvelous occasion as this. Please, I insist that you make your way up here." He motioned them further into the arena space, where the balloon was almost completely filled, and gave Margaret a wink as he headed off to say "farewell" to his family.

She felt her heartbeat pounding like a drum inside her ears at what just happened. Her mind was still processing the fact that Mr. Wise noticed her amongst the ensuing crowd of onlookers. Though it was for a mere second of a facial expression, Margaret Everton had finally met him face-to-face! This moment was one she promised to cherish as long as she lived, and into the next life beyond that. *I wish I could go up in the balloon with him. The view must be incredible!*

Many watched the famed aeronaut console his wife, and six-year-old son, that he would be gone no longer than half the day, before he bravely stepped into the small basket with an unwavering sense of confidence. Margaret observed his procedure of checking his few belongings, confirming that the ballasts had been firmly attached, and then said "all is right." The men holding on to the leading ropes released the tension, allowing the balloon to slowly lift from terra firma, and succumb to the unknown far above.

As Mr. Wise continued to display an adventurous calm, people hollered and cheered with applause at a deafening level of sound. The entire square was swept up in a tidal wave of excitement, overpowering the band playing inspirational tunes in vain. A joyful praise rang out unanimously for the man who dared to float into the heavenly landscape of clouds where humans had not tread until now. But no one shouted with more enthusiasm than that of Margaret; who cared not for decorum in the face of so much wonder. She waved so fast that her arm was ready to fall, and her eyes remained glued to the basket, unwilling to look away until he vanished beyond sight.

Pretty soon, the hands on the clock tower revealed that another ten minutes had passed before the spectators began to empty the once crowded square for other endeavors. As the aeronaut's balloon, the "Aerial," climbed further and farther above Carlisle, Mr. Wise would peer back every few minutes or so, tipping his hat to those still watching through the use of telescopes.

It was at this time, however, that Reverend Thorn approached Margaret with another set of twinkles in his eyes, with his paper and pencil still in hand. "Is this not the most amazing thing you have ever seen?"

"He still has to reach a higher level if he wants to ride the faster streams of wind that will carry him easterly." She stated. Margaret knew that there were countless issues that might occur when being a mile-high in the air: the seams of the balloon could allow the gas to escape due to any unforeseen weaknesses in the stitching and lacquer process, an abnormal gust of wind could send him frightfully off-course, not to mention the affects that varying temperatures had on the gaseous properties of the hydrogen he used. Of course, all of her knowledge was obtained from second-hand accounts, and articles based on Mr. Wise's previous accessions; considering the fact that she had no money to spend on such expensive materials herself. "I wonder how far he can see at that height."

"Well, given how clear the sky is, I imagine New Jersey is in view from up there!" The reverend speculated. "Here." He politely asked one of the men, from his church, to allow Margaret to peak through the lens of his telescope. "Through another's eyes, we can see a whole new world ahead."

Margaret gratefully accepted the offer, and peered up to see the balloon shrinking in size against the vast blue of the sky. But that was not all she saw. Mr. Wise's placid composure was suddenly gone, and his arms were spread out like an eagle's wings, attempting to signal someone on the ground below. His mouth was moving, shouting out a message that was inaudible to those in the square. "I think something is wrong."

"Pardon?" The reverend asked.

She continued to use the telescope, noticing the man wildly pointing in the direction of St. John's Church; even removing his hat in order to wave it like a flag. Pulling her eyes away from the lens, Margaret flashed a concerned look at Reverend Thorn. "Mr. Wise is upset about something happening over there." Taking note of the church's tall steeple on the north-eastern side of the square, Margaret's gaze fell upon the structure next to it. The bricked, two-story building would have passed for an ordinary house, if it had not been for the extra bars protecting the windows and front door. "What is in that building to the left of the church?"

"It's the bank." Reverend Thorn answered, suddenly finding himself attempting to juggle the telescope Margaret hastily shoved into his hands. She sprinted across the lawn, while the band played on, and raced over Hanover Street.

Mrs. McKnee, who had been discussing some alterations with the blonde-haired seamstress, abruptly turned around at the sound of Margaret fleeing the area. She called out to her twice before taking up pursuit along the bricked sidewalk, and was immediately stopped in a stream of people moving at a leisurely pace. But Miss Everton was already at the corner of the church, peering down the side street adjoining onto Mulberry Alley. There, in-between the two large structures stood a man with a brown hat and his face angled away from the main street.

And just who are you? Margaret thought to herself.

With his back to her, the man whispered something through the secondary door of the bank, and then hunched over a small object near the ground. From what she could see, his coat was a riddle of patches featuring all sorts of colors and patterns, his boots were in desperate need of resoling by the cobbler, and his hat contained animal bite marks along the brim. Almost everything about his appearance seemed to indicate that he had been out of work for some time. That was until she caught sight of the shiny gun he carried on his hip. It was undeniably a revolver, that Margaret surmised to have .31 or .34 caliber bullets in its chambers. Having recognized it as one of the models her father special-ordered in for Coon, there was a brief second when she feared it to be him; despite this man being half her friend's age.

As the man turned around, Margaret recoiled back and overheard his next words to the person standing behind the door, from inside the bank. "Alright! I just hope that Jerry did his part! Now step away, will ya?!" He coughed into sooty hands, and struck a match against the brick wall just as she dared to look again. Margaret's eyes suddenly grew large and she dove behind the corner of the church once more with only a second to spare.

An abrupt explosion rocked the ground and split the friendly air into a heart pounding standstill. It did not take long for the man's partner to burst through the new opening with sacks of money in his hands, and the two thieves began to make their escape, just as Kathleen grabbed ahold of Margaret. "Are you alright?"

"Yes! But those men are robbing the bank!"

By now, several people had already gathered where Margaret stood, blankly staring at the newly-blasted hole as a bank employee rushed out of the building to fetch the sheriff. One of the men who recently joined the group, had a gun himself, and fired three shots at the robbers as they mounted their horses. The scene soon descended into chaos as others went inside the bank to check if anyone else was hurt. While Margaret and Kathleen talked about what she had heard right before the explosion, the bank manager cautiously stepped out and over the broken wood through the help of another teller.

He was a tall and thin older gentleman, wearing a tan suit with black shoes, and a fresh bump which was quite noticeable at the base of his skull. Having woken up after being knocked out by the robbers, his footing was shaky at best, and he held a hand up to shield his eyes from the bright sunlight. "Did...did..."

"Wilfred went to get help. But you need to see the doctor." The teller answered. He brought the manager to the sidewalk and propped his throbbing head against the brick wall.

A tavern owner was the first to ask the obvious question, one of which none of them were anxious to have the answer too. "How much did they steal?"

"Ten thousand dollars." The manager's unsteady reply was met with a collective gasp from the crowd.

"They came in and demanded we open the safe to fill their bags." The teller continued on with the story, filling in for his injured boss who was trying to silence an unrelenting headache. "When Mr. Arnold refused to oblige their request, he received a hit on the head and was knocked unconscious for a while. Wilfred and I did what they asked, thinking they would leave as soon as we finished stuffing the bags. But they held us until the door exploded only minutes ago."

"I thought the bank was closing at eleven today?" Someone else chimed in from the back row.

"We were about to lock up when the three of them entered the building and threatened us at gunpoint."

"There were three of them?" The sheriff slowed his run down to a walk as he started to inspect the damage. Wilfred was not far behind, struggling to catch his breath from locating the sheriff outside the Mansion Hotel. "Which direction did they go?"

"Down the alley!" A couple members of the crowd shouted almost in unison. "Is someone going to go after them, Sheriff?!"

Towering over nearly all of the surrounding townsfolk by a good twelve inches in height, the sheriff commanded the audience's attention with a simple stare. "I am going to do the best I can. Now, if…"

"Sheriff! We have one! We got him, Sheriff!" Came the shouts of four men who had gone inside the bank after the blast first occurred. The growing crowd, including Margaret and Kathleen, waited with bated breath to see who they had supposedly captured. "We have him caught in his own trap! Yes, we sure do!"

The Sheriff's face smirked when he recognized the man they pulled outside the busted building. Walking under his own admission, but clearly ready to run at a moment's notice, was a chestnut brown-haired young man wearing a blue suit and a pair of inexpensive shoes. "I should have known! Well, it appears that you won't be able to talk your-self out of this one, Gerome Wellington."

"That's the one who entered the bank with the two high-waymen!" The teller exclaimed, pointing madly at the blue-suited individual.

"Sheriff, I had nothing to do with any of this!" Mr. Wel-lington defended, finally ripping his arms free of the small group's restraint, and holding them up in a protest of inno-cence. "I barely know those men, and was taken captive, same as the others."

"And why do I find that difficult to believe?" The sher-iff's expression hardened as he spoke. "Better tell us all where your friends are headed, Gerome. The judge might even spare your life, if you cooperate. Though, he might have already spent all of his charitable will last time."

Margaret was about to inch forward, attempting to gain an unobstructed view of the accused man, when her father called out her name and wrapped her in a loving embrace. "There you are! I was on my way back to the hotel when Martin found me on the sidewalk, and said you were still in the square with Kathleen."

Martin McKnee, who was right on Thomas's heels, also gave his wife a short hug, pleased to find that she had not been hurt in the explosion. "I was coming out to find you at the time that…" His eyes glanced over at the hole in the bank's wall and the worsening crowd that was calling for Mr. Wellington's head. "Gerome?"

"You have one last chance to confess to the crime, MR. WELLINGTON!" The sheriff demanded in a sharp tone of voice.

"I DID NOT DO IT!"

"WHERE ARE THEY GOING WITH THE MONEY?!"

Mr. Wellington tried to contain the ensuing anger boiling in his blood. "Sheriff, honestly, I…"

"Honestly? I would not wager that to be a word in your vocabulary, Gerome. Since it is clear that you are not going to be helpful in this matter, you are coming with me!" Pulling a pair of handcuffs from his belt, the sheriff clasped them around the man's wrists and gave him a bone-chilling look that seared through his skin. "Today is your lucky day, Mr. Wellington; because you just bought yourself a permanent excuse from class."

CHAPTER 5

Martin stopped the sheriff in his tracks, and offered to personally vouch for Mr. Wellington's character to keep him from the jailhouse. "Gerome could not commit a bank robbery, Sheriff. You know, as well as I, that he is studying to become a financial lawyer. Why would he take that risk when graduation is so close?"

"Perhaps he cannot afford to pay off his tuition, and was relying on citizens with good-standing, such as your-self, to protect him, like you are now." Their stares became locked in an unyielding battle as Mr. McKnee and the sher-iff exchanged silent threats.

Gerome tipped his head at Kathleen's husband in a ges-ture of gratitude. "Thank you, Mr. McKnee, but I do not want you to be taken down because of me. I will be alright."

"This is lunacy, Gerome! You are innocent, for that I am certain!" Martin's face was hot with frustration, sending daggers at the sheriff who few dared to challenge. "Admit it! You have been after him for years, and are blinded by your own hatred! So instead of gathering together a posse, and chasing after the real thieves, you are going to accuse the wrong person and…"

"If this college student is anything, Mr. McKnee, it is NOT innocent!" The sheriff puffed out his chest and shouted his voice louder than a cannon. "Might I suggest you keep your anger in check for your own fight, McKnee. Because if I find out that you are in cahoots with this robbery, there will be no crevice big enough for you to hide in. Mark my words!" Pulling the law student toward the jail on Hanover Street, the sheriff instructed a part-time deputy to round up a number of men, and form a posse to chase after the robbers.

Margaret managed to overhear Mr. Wellington deny any involvement for one final time, as Thomas drew her away from his chest and the sheriff moved his prisoner swiftly out of sight. "Please tell me you were not near the bank when the robbers escaped."

"But I did see it, Father. And I heard one of the men say the name 'Jerry' right before he blasted the door open." She boldly answered, knowing full well that he'd probably be outraged at discovering how close she truly had been.

"Did the men see you?" Her father's concerned voice shook her nerves a little. His wife had insisted that Coon's stories were planting too many adventurous thoughts in their daughter's brain, and now he wondered if she had been right all along.

"No. I think not. Where were you when it happened?"

"I saw it from behind St. John's. Mr. Guthrie and I returned from the square, and we were talking inside his shop, when we heard the explosion. All we could see where their backs as they mounted and raced away."

"The bank manager said that they took ten thousand dollars, but I don't think they were highwaymen, like the teller claims they were." Margaret told her father, who was intently listening to her every word. "For one thing, highwaymen would not venture toward the centre of town with so many people roaming the sidewalks. And remember what that couple said last month, the ones who stayed overnight from New York, and were on their way to Virginia? The men who stopped them said 'stand and deliver,' which matches with Coon's stories."

"Margaret, a few men not saying a common phrase does not disprove them as highwaymen. There is no limit to what desperate people will do when they have nothing left to lose."

"Why do you say that, Father?" Although Margaret had not mentioned about the man's poor house appearance, Thomas's eyes carried a note of secrecy; as she could tell he was withholding something from her.

"One of the robbers had a shiny revolver on his hip. I only caught a glimpse of the sun's reflection from its metal surface. But Mr. Guthrie rushed out before I had, and noticed something familiar about him." Her father was about to continue until a member of the crowd approached them with a curious expression on his face.

"I apologize for listening to your conversation, Mister. However, did I hear you correctly that James Guthrie might know one of the highwaymen?" The stranger's voice caught the attention of a few other people still in the square, and they all turned to face Mr. Everton with inquisitive looks of their own.

"I do not believe Mr. Guthrie knows the man in the same sense that one does a friend or relative. He only mentioned that he entered his shop two days prior to today, and asked if he could fix a mechanical issue in the weapon. He offered to pay Mr. Guthrie in poultry, and his last box of cigarettes. When Mr. Guthrie refused, on the grounds that he felt something bad would come of his help, the man left with an angry scowl on his face. I suppose he was right, given what just happened and all."

"That would explain why the man did not fire back during their escape, when someone shot at them. Maybe that also explains why they used explosives to take out the side door. Although, I rather think that has more to do with what the man used to do for a living, than his gun not working properly." Margaret added, much to the surprise of the surrounding people.

"What do you mean?" Thomas asked his daughter.

"The man who said 'Jerry' wore clothes that were more akin to rags than actual garments, and he coughed into his sooty hands as he talked. He also showed his experience using explosives in a skilled manner, so it is a reasonable guess that he worked in a coal mining town until recently." Margaret observed her father's blank stare and went on even further. "In Scotland, a number of physicians have stated that there is a direct line between the coal mining dust they inhale, and the deterioration of the workers' health. Our 'neighbor' had information on it in one of his books." It was a mutually understood agreement between their wealthier neighbor, and the residents of Meyer's Bend, that no one was to say his name outside of their village. His seasonal escape was a safe haven only if it remained a secret from others, and he treated the residents well in return for their silence.

Though no one else had a clue of who she was eluding to, Thomas figured it out and felt his fear only strengthening. For his daughter to have seen all of these details, she had been closer to the robbery than he first realized. And if her conclusions were correct, then these men were different from average robbers. *What if they come back looking for her? Margaret would be able to identify them, and...and...*

"Are you certain that neither one of them saw you?"

"He was focused on using the dynamite. I am sure he did not see me." Margaret wanted to keep her father from worrying about her; especially since his doubts were now crossing into her own mind.

"Perhaps we should continue this conversation in a more private setting." Kathleen suggested, watching the crowd growing more agitated as time progressed. While some of the original on-lookers had grown tiresome and left for other destinations, there was no telling what might happen next.

"I believe the woman is right, Sir." The stranger agreed with Mrs. McKnee in a casual tone. "You should also tell your suspicions to the sheriff, after he is done arresting Mr. Wellington."

"Ever always the helper, huh…Ace Highsmith." A different townsman stepped forth in a morning suit and matching hat, shifting his weight onto his left leg as he spoke. "You would not be using this opportunity to get ahead in public opinion for election day, now would ya?"

I've heard that name before, Margaret thought to herself, *but where?*

"One would think that sneaky of a trick could only be capable of you, Donald Sutherby." Ace stood approximately six inches shorter than his counterpart, and had a bare face in comparison to Mr. Sutherby's beard and mustache. But the thick facial hair did little to cover up the other man's dislike for Ace's comment, and a few of his friends started chanting for a fight.

Mr. McKnee quickly took a strong stance in the middle of the semi-circle that had suddenly formed around them, wanting to head off any potential trouble. "Alright you two. That's enough jabbering while the robbers are still on the move with our town's money. Now, I am going to hire a lawyer for Mr. Wellington, and find out what charges the Sheriff intends holding him on for the time being. If you two would like to demonstrate your ability for action, then might I suggest joining the posse that the Deputy is establishing."

"We should double the night watch efforts as well." Mr. Sutherby stated, hearing the snickering from someone deeper in the crowd.

"You never work your night anyways, and pay that drunkard from Three Jolly Irishmen to take your place!"

"I do not!"

"ENOUGH!" Martin shouted for everyone to quiet down. "Return to your own businesses, and let us try to get things back to normal as best we can." In a bitter silence, many of the group finally began to disperse just as a nine-year-old boy ran up to Mr. McKnee in a frightful hurry and asked for the sheriff. "What is it, Bobby?"

"At the Mansion Hotel, Mr. Adler has been murdered!"

CHAPTER 6

Mr. Adler had been a man nearing the ripe age of for-ty-five. He was one of the few hotel workers who had access to the safe in the main office, and was a father of two kids with his wife, Wendy. On various days of the week, regard-less of sunshine or snow, Wendy would sell handmade items at the market-house, and cook her husband's favorite meal on Sundays; chicken and dumplings. The same man who also happened to be lying dead on the office floor, in front of the open safe with a nearly emptied inner shelf.

The sheriff stood there, observing the scene that was clearly upsetting the hotel manager to his right. "Gene, you better close the lobby for now. No one goes out or comes in until I say so, ya hear?"

Quietly nodding in agreement, Gene Moore ushered his guests to their rooms, and instructed his employees to close the bar, kitchen, and parlor rooms without an explana-tion. Unfortunately, the few patrons at the bar were already sleeping off their drinks, leaving the staff the thankless task of moving them against their will.

Mr. McKnee insisted on staying in the lobby, as it was one of his company's safes that had been broken into, and he wished to inspect the damage. "Kathleen, you take Margaret and Thomas to our room, and I promise to have the sheriff come up for their statements a little later in the day."

"I really should get back home to tell Nancy what happened. I shall see to it this instant." Mr. Everton added. "If we do not arrive in Meyer's Bend by nightfall, she will be worried sick about us."

"Then we best have you two tell him your statements now." Martin walked toward the main office as his wife sat down in a red upholstered chair near the front door. Her face was sullen from the horrible afternoon, touching her forehead with the tip of her finger to move a stray hair from her eyes.

"Unbelievable. Simply unheard of in this town. Some rioting and bar fights, sure. But a bank robbery and a murder in the same day? Within a couple hours of one another, even. What is happening to Carlisle?"

Margaret thought back to the heated discussion that transpired between the sheriff and Martin in the town square. *I wonder...* "Is there any reason that the sheriff would suspect your husband as being a part of the robbery?"

"Well, the bank did turn down purchasing a newer safe from Martin's company four days ago. They have an older model from a manufacturer that is no more, and he was going to issue them a discount for trying out the latest lock system. It is designed to prevent thieves from being able to access anything without the key. However, I do not think it would have changed today's outcome, if they had decided to install the new safe. With the bank manager unconscious, the key was practically given to them."

"And how old is this hotel's safe?"

"An original model, from Martin's earlier days in the company…" Kathleen's face suddenly widened as an idea came to her. "Although…" She slowly stopped herself from saying another word with so many ears being present.

"Margaret, you are not implying that Martin had anything to do with this?!" Her father strongly cautioned her with the glare in his eyes.

"No, of course not."

"But, the hotel recently rejected to buy a version of the newer lock as well." Kathleen reluctantly decided to say aloud, switching her worried gaze between the two Evertons. "We might need a lawyer of our own."

"A few businesses who did not buy a safe from Martin's company is not evidence of a crime. There are probably others who also said no at some point, without anything bad happening to them." Thomas interjected. "It is most certainly a mere coincidence."

His daughter tilted her head in thought. "Possibly. However, I am fairly confident that Mr. Wellington is innocent, and the sheriff appears to have an issue with both him and Mr. McKnee. What is there to stop him from charging both men in the hopes that at least one will fall?" Margaret glanced hopefully over at her mother's friend for some answers. "What does he have against them?"

"Martin inadvertently caused his son's company to foreclose, nearly sending him into the poor house. Gerome, on the other hand, broke off his engagement to the sheriff's daughter at the sheriff's own request. And before you ask, he still holds a grudge that his daughter remains loyal to Gerome and will not speak to him until he allows them to wed."

Margaret was shocked, to say the least. "That was more than I was expecting."

"Gerome does enjoy 'tempting fate' if you will. He likes to push the fence and see if it breaks, relying on his wits to save him from a prison sentence. It has been known to get him into trouble at the college, with the overly-confident attitude he can sometimes have. But a robbery is beyond the line he dares to tread." Kathleen stared at her hands, shaking from the events of the last few hours. "Imagine. The clock has barely struck three thirty, and the day feels like an uncontrollable nightmare." She looked up at Margaret with eyes glassy from the emotions swirling in her own brain. "Poor Gene. His wife is the sheriff's sister, you know. She wanted to marry a man who preferred a less adventurous job in life. And yet here we are, with a cruel twist of destiny; where he was almost killed by a thief himself."

Wanting to see more of where the hotel worker had died, Margaret thought of a topic that would easily distract her father and Kathleen. Once she had them discussing what the perfect present would be for her mother's upcoming birthday, Margaret took the opportunity to steadily inch her way closer to the main office's threshold, and peered around Martin to see inside.

The sheriff was still combing through the area with determination in his gaze, waiting for the hotel manager to assess all that was missing from the safe. Though the room was not grand, by any means, it still held a fairly large mahoganyized desk, a cushioned chair, and a small set of book shelves running along the far wall. She could see that Mr. Adler's head had been bashed in by a blunt object, while the poor man lay flat between the desk and the opened safe. The only shelf in the black and grey metal box, had but one object still resting inside, and it was the most stumper of a puzzle indeed.

"I think I have a full inventory of what's been taken." Mr. Moore handed over a piece of paper with a list of items written on it to the sheriff to see. His face was weary with dread, having the burden of finding his devoted employee dead in his own office. A bead of sweat fell down his forehead, as his nerves were becoming overloaded with the mounting stress of it all. "We do not usually keep so much cash on hand, but with the balloon ascension today, and the families visiting the college, our rooms have been filled this entire past week."

"A few pieces of jewelry, a deposit for the bank, some checks for a Mr. Klondike, a pair of cufflinks, and…what was in the box registered to…a…Mr. Thurber?" The sheriff tapped his finger next to the penciled entry on the paper.

"No idea. He said that while it did not contain anything harmful, we were not to open it so long as he is a guest in the hotel." Mr. Moore's hands were beginning to shake now, staring at the lifeless body of his former bookkeeper on the ground. "Do you think…"

The sheriff placed a consoling hand on his brother-in-law, and locked eyes with him in an effort to steady the man's thoughts. "Whatever happened here, Gene, the responsibility does not fall on your shoulders. Understand?" He waited for the manager to verbally agree, before glancing over to find Margaret standing behind Mr. McKnee, just outside the main office door. "And what are you doing in the lobby? Get that girl out of here!"

Martin turned around to see the blur of Margaret dashing back to where her father was still chatting with Kathleen in the lobby, and shook his head in jest. "That would be Miss Everton, who was a witness to the bank robbery earlier today. Her father, Thomas, also has a statement to make."

"A witness? What exactly did she see?"

"You would have to ask her that yourself, Sheriff. I would not want to hamper the process of justice by tainting anything she has to say."

Squinting his eyes at Martin, the sheriff stared long and hard at him. "How exactly is this 'Miss Everton' connected to you, Mr. McKnee? Did you pay her so she could protect your friend, Mr. Wellington?"

"If I did not know you better, Sheriff, I would have taken high offense to that insinuation. Her mother happens to be a childhood friend of my wife's. They are in town today for the ascension, as well as a few business matters."

"I will have my other deputy take their statements when he comes on duty. I have no time for your blatant attempts at misdirection on this case."

Martin scoffed at the air, frustrated by the sheriff's mutually stubborn nature. "As if I personally arranged for all of this to happen? Oh, Sheriff, you flatter me so. Some brains, I do admittedly have, but not for such an implausible plan you believe I created. For what was my motive? Hmm? What would I have to gain from such a scheme?"

The sheriff smirked with a mischievous glint in his pupils, and was clearly going to enjoy what he had to say next. "Between you and me, McKnee, there is only one of us who has a past of taking out his rage through murderous intent."

Martin's face failed to hide his surprise at the partially-veiled threat he had just been given. His mind spun with the tales of yesteryear, from that haunted day he assumed was buried six-feet under, and no one else the wiser. "There is no possible way for you to have knowledge of something that did not happen."

"Oh, allow me to put your fears to rest, Mr. McKnee. I happen to have first-hand knowledge about your little business deal that went bad up north. I dare not speak of such matters where the public is concerned, until the appropriate time should come to pass. So if I were you, I would keep the witless remarks to a minimum. Hmm?" Picking up the cigar case that remained inside the safe, the sheriff pointed to the engraved initials on the front of the shiny box. "Seems to me that those there letters are M.M. Hmm. Don't you consider it quite puzzling to find this as the sole item left behind by the thieves?"

Martin's bottom lip slightly quivered as he straightened his back, and pulled his jacket taunt with his hands. "I admit that it is mine. Though I have no idea why the thieves did not take it, except to say," he cleared his throat, "that is the honest truth, Sheriff. Now, if you excuse me, Thomas and Margaret will be leaving for home soon, and I shall neglect them no longer." Briskly returning to the lobby where the others were still waiting, Martin hastily ushered them upstairs as the sheriff watched from the office below. There was no telling what the lawman had up his sleeves, and time was running out.

CHAPTER 7

"What do you mean we should go home and forget what we saw?!" Margaret was shocked by Mr. McKnee's sudden change in attitude as they reached the hotel room. "I thought Gerome was your friend?"

She was about to say something else, when Thomas calmly placed a firm hand on his daughter's shoulder, silently instructing her to lower her tone. "Are you certain that is what you want?"

"I have retained a lawyer for Mr. Wellington, and will most likely have to do so for myself, given the sheriff's current position on the matter at hand. I have faith that we will prevail in the court systems, and…and…wish you both a safe journey home." Martin's lips were stiff, his stance rigid, and his eyes nervously flickered from window to window out of pure fear alone. Instantly, Kathleen knew that something was amiss, and she demanded for her husband to tell her what the sheriff had said. But Martin brushed off her concerns with a false sense of indifference. "Ridiculous notion. He told me nothing to alter my opinions. The sheriff is simply doing his job to find out who is responsible for Mr. Adler's death."

Kathleen was far from convinced due to his lack of conviction, and was not about to allow the Evertons to leave town before she knew their lives were out of harm's way. She had never known anything that would cause her husband to shrink like a violet, and the thought of it was enough to scare herself into hiding. "Martin, this is not like you! I am no lunkhead, and most assuredly not blind. He talked with you in the office, we all heard the whispers, and Margaret said…"

"She needs to keep her observations to herself! That is what any well-mannered child would do!" Martin snapped, much to his own wife's bewilderment.

"Thomas, I think you better take Margaret outside for now." Kathleen gave the girl a reassuring wink as they left the room, and closed the door behind them.

Standing awkwardly in the middle of the hallway was bad enough, without the added ability of hearing the harsh words being shouted from within the McKnee's room. Margaret felt the weight of shameful guilt suddenly plague her mind, and she asked her father if they could venture downstairs instead. Happy to give the McKnees more privacy, Thomas led his daughter toward the staircase once again, in search of one of the parlor rooms on the first floor.

If the day's sun had not been still hanging outside a nearby window, one would have sworn it was midnight at the hotel. The echoes of their footsteps helped to fill the otherwise silent building that would have rivaled a cemetery, and the small clock near the check-in counter ticked away the minutes like a thief in the dark. Her father's hands were beginning to sweat in part from the new worries now crowding his head, causing some tension to enter the air as well. Neither of them dared to speak a word until they reached the door to the office, and Thomas asked the sheriff if they could stay in the parlor room. After a gruff wave of his hand in dismissal, Mr. Moore pulled a key from his vest pocket and handed it to the hotel worker named Frederick.

Having spent time with her wealthiest neighbor, on both weekends and weekdays, Margaret had seen how maids, and low-level workers, were often ignored by those residing in the higher social classes. Although her friend treated his servants with kindness and due-earned respect, a few of his associates were far less considerate when they visited on occasion. To many of them, servants were not even there until they were in need of their services. *I wonder how much he knows?* She looked at the younger man walking them across the floor, and waited for him to turn the key in the lock, before she asked. "It is Frederick, right?"

"Yes, Miss." The worker's face displayed his pleasant surprise at hearing her say his name. "You were visiting with Mr. and Mrs. McKnee, I believe?"

"That we are. Kathleen, Mrs. McKnee, is a friend of my mother's." Margaret quietly closed the door behind them, and peeked through the crack near the lock, to ensure no one had been watching. *Here's to hoping I know what I am about to do.* Glancing up at the tall, slender worker, she told herself to act as though he was a traveler at their store, and slowly inhaled. "Frederick, I will understand if you do not wish to say anything, since we are mere strangers to you, but we could use your help. Mr. McKnee might be in trouble, and while we believe him to be innocent, the sheriff holds a different view. Is there anything you saw, or heard, that could help us clear him of those suspicions?"

Frederick stared at his hands, playing with his fingers like they were scattering mice in a barn. "I'm really not supposed to talk about the guests, Miss. The McKnees have treated me well though…have truly been good to me, you might say." His head shook from side to side in a frightful manner. "But this job is all I have. Without it…"

Thomas decided to step in, and gave the worker an encouraging smile. "It is alright, Frederick. You do not have to tell us. A man has to protect himself in life, and we understand that." Although Mr. Everton had to admit that his own curiosity wished to hear what he knew, it would not serve anyone by forcing the man to speak.

"Thank you, Sir. That is mighty kind of you. Mr. Adler, he was a fair person too. An honest man, with a name that should not be smeared in any way. No, Sir." Frederick surveyed the entire space before motioning for them to come in closer, so they could whisper. "Mr. Moore owes money to a number of people. One of them has a temper that can possess him to do terrible things. He beats up men with unpayable debts, and sometimes takes their possessions as payment."

Margaret's thoughts sprang back to the short conversation the sheriff had with his brother-in-law in the office. "Is that why Mr. Moore believes Adler's death is his fault?"

Frederick quickly nodded. "Mr. Moore thinks he is untouchable because his wife is the sheriff's sister. So he goes around to different poker games and bets more than he has. I know this because I accidently saw him at one of those games in this very hotel, and was told to forget about it. After I saw the men leave the next morning, Mr. Moore was practically in tears, and that same man was threatening him on the second floor."

"Who does he owe, Frederick?" Thomas politely asked, eager to learn of the man's identity.

"Mr. Sutherby." Frederick signaled to them that he was done talking, and hastily left the parlor room to return to the office.

CHAPTER 8

"This whole thing stinks worse than spoiled fish." Thomas sat next to the window and peered outside at the wagons going down the road beside the hotel. The sidewalks were practically empty, except for a few stranglers here and there. *How odd to think that the rest of the world continues to spin, whilst we are stuck like lifeless dolls inside a playhouse prison.*

"Martin seemed to be familiar with both Ace Highsmith and Donald Sutherby when we were at the square." Margaret paced back and forth along the same line on the floorboards. "I believe he mentioned something about an election? And I know I recognize Mr. Highsmith's name. Though I cannot be sure from where." She suddenly snapped her fingers as she remembered. "That's it! The sheriff's election! I read his name in the newspaper, and if I recall correctly, there are over ten men running for the that position this year. Perhaps Mr. Sutherby felt that it was safe to collect what was owed to him, given that Mr. Moore's brother-in-law is on the way out."

"That is *if* Frederick is even correct in what he told us. Sometimes, you are too trustworthy of others, Margaret. Or have you forgotten what Sue Ellen tricked you into buying from her last month?" Her father raised a brow as he cast her a cautionary look.

Margaret rolled her eyes. "No, Father. How could I, after she said those seeds would grow into Germany Tea Leaves. At the very minimum, she might have sold me seeds that actually grew into *some* kind of a plant!" She plopped into a chair opposite of where he sat, squinting her eyes against the bright sunlight and thinking aloud for a moment. "I wonder just what the sheriff does have on Martin."

Thomas instantly recognized the glint in his daughter's eyes, and picked up on the notes of excitement sprinkled in her words. She always did cherish a good puzzle; exercising her brain was a daily enjoyment for his little girl. But it was the same glint in those pupils that led to the flying machine in their barn, and the same glint that also resulted in her reading a record of fifteen books in a single week. Once her mind was set on a determined path, there was no hope of stopping her. But he had to try this time.

Raising a hand into the air, Thomas attempted to persuade his daughter into dropping the matter altogether. "Margaret, as much as this is a tempting riddle to solve, I feel that it is only my duty to warn you of the risks involved when stepping into other's affairs. It is commendable of you to want to do the right thing; however, life is not cut-and-dry, and…"

"How many times did we ask for someone to help William? Hmm?" As she interrupted her father, even Margaret was a little shocked at her harsh tone. Despite the countless number of times she told herself to leave their cousin's tragic fate in the past, she could not remove what happened from her mind. "We asked, begged, and pleaded with others to come forth, and none of them ever did. They were all too scared, Father."

"I know, I was there too." Thomas had always felt sorry for what his wife's cousin had endured, and some nights pondered if there was more he might have been able to do to change the outcome. After William had been unjustly sentenced to prison, by a biased group of jury members, their cousin was killed during a riot, and his body laid to rest in an unmarked grave. But no matter how fond they all had been of William, Margaret was Thomas's only child, and he promised to protect her ever since she was born. *I could not bear it if something were to happen to her.*

Margaret sensed his deep concern, and silently sat down beside him on the couch, with the most sweet and sincere smile spread wide across her lips. "Father, Kathleen has been so nice to us, and if Martin is involved in these crimes, she has no one else to turn to for help. We are the closest thing to relatives she has in this world, and I could not live with myself if the wrong man lost his life again when I had the chance to do something about it."

Mr. Everton slowly nodded before giving his daughter a loving kiss on the forehead, reluctantly agreeing with her that turning to run was no longer an option. "Alright. I'll go along with you on this, under one condition. We investigate the matter smartly, and not through brazen actions."

"Fair enough." Margaret extended her arms to give him a hug, when a loud banging noise rang out from the hotel's front door. Both Evertons shot upright and rushed to the parlor's threshold, where they watched Frederick cautiously open the door. Immediately, a small group of people were trying to push and shove their way into the hotel against Frederick's hidden strength.

As the sheriff raced out from the office, Thomas pulled their door almost shut, so they could look on from the shadows. "What's all this commotion about?"

"We want to know why you are not out with the posse, Sheriff?!" A young reporter demanded, using his elbows to fight off a man half his height.

"Is there any truth to the rumor that Mr. Adler has been killed, Sheriff?"

"Yay! We want to know if the two incidents are connected!"

It was an interesting site to behold, as each of the newspaper reporters, even one stating he was from the Shippensburg area, nearly wrestled for the same lines the sheriff was to give them all. "Now see here, you know that I cannot divulge the information until we are certain of the basic facts. I am here to handle the matters within the town's limits, while my deputy is managing the posse that is hunting down the robbers, as we speak." Just as he was about to close the door in the reporters' faces, a familiar member of the crowd quickly slipped inside, and the sheriff greeted him like an old friend. "Ace? I thought you'd be out after the thieves with the others."

"Sutherby went along with the group, so I decided it was best I stayed in town. Say, what did happen to Adler? Bobby was spotted running by the Quinn's house, and those vultures swooped in for the story."

"That explains it." The sheriff rubbed his forehead and tipped his hat back, exposing a sweaty tuff of black hair underneath. "Adler appears to have been killed in the hotel's office, before his killer stole almost everything from the safe."

Ace was speechless for a momentary heartbeat, giving himself time to comprehend what occurred. "What was left behind?"

"A cigar case with Martin McKnee's initials engraved

upon its surface."

"Wait, it was my understanding that Adler had off on Saturdays."

"Normally, he does. Given how filled the hotel's register is, however, Gene asked him to come in today." The sheriff continued to describe how he believed the murder took place, while Margaret and her father listened in from the parlor room. "Gene was tending to an issue with a guest's horse, when Adler entered the office to begin calculating the books. The killer walked in through the office's only door, and forced Adler to open the safe. Once it was unlocked, he struck him down with an object…of some kind…and then took everything he could."

"Except the expensive cigar case?" Ace seemed a little skeptical at the sheriff's theory.

"It would be more recognizable with the initials, and therefore, harder to sell off. Perhaps that is the reason it was not taken. The fatal blow came from behind, on the back of his skull, that much I'm certain."

"Do you think there is any connection between the two events?"

The sheriff shrugged his shoulders. "Your guess is as good as mine. I was hoping that Quinn would be here by now to collect his body, before I go around to see if one of the other guests saw anything."

Ace slowly shifted his chin upward, watching the sheriff through his now squinted eyes. "Delaying the task of having to tell his wife and children?"

"You, of all people, understand that horror. The longer I wait, is another minute they have to carry a smile on their faces." Kicking a piece of mud away from the bottom of his boots, the sheriff scoffed into the air. "The rumors will most likely reach them now, with those…" His scowl quickly turned into a smile of relief, at seeing the gravedigger being admitted into the hotel by Frederick. "Finally. I was wondering when you would show up."

Ace opened his mouth to speak, but hastily closed it again; waiting for a pause in their conversation to ask what was on his mind. "Sheriff, what about the girl and her father, from the square? They were accompanied by Mr. McKnee and his wife, and I believe they were witnesses to the robbery."

"Yeah, Martin already informed me that they have statements I should hear." The sheriff looked up from watching Quinn take the deceased man's measurements for the coffin. "Martin is my prime suspect at the present time, so I do not place their testimony very high on my list. But to be on the safe side, I would consider it a personal favor if you acted as their security escort until they leave town."

"Surely there is no reason for Martin McKnee to go after his own friends." Ace pulled his brown hat down to smooth out a strange fold in the brim. "Could it be that your view is tainted…due to who is involved?"

"No more than yours when it comes to the Adlers." The sheriff pulled him aside, shielding what he was about to say from Gene, standing behind the counter. He even lowered the tone of his voice, making it more difficult for the Evertons to hear everything that was being said. "My gut tells me that you want to assist in the investigation. But I think you would be more useful in guarding the girl and her father. If I allow you to get closer to this case, all of the other contenders for my position will be screaming that they were not given the same opportunity. And we both know that Sutherby would be first in line."

The two men shared a mutual chuckle at the mention of Sutherby's name, and Ace did his best at hiding the disappointment he truly felt. "You have my word. I want this solved as much as you do." Moving his gaze from side to side, Ace asked the sheriff where the witnesses were in the hotel.

"Over in the first parlor room. I gave Frederick the permission to unlock it." He pointed to the door absent-mindedly, not noticing that it had been left slightly open the entire time. "Report to me when they decide to leave Carlisle."

"Yes, Sir."

CHAPTER 9

Margaret quickly sat in the nearest chair to her left, whilst her father calmly walked toward the centre of the room. Her butt had barely enough time to touch the seat, when Ace walked through the door, after hesitating near the entrance from seeing it open. She gave him a short smile and leaned into her charm, like she normally did with Coon back home. "You were in the square earlier. Mr. Highsmith, I presume?"

"Yes, I am. Though, I do regret for having rudely spied on the private conversation you had with your father earlier. Eavesdropping is not considered to be polite behavior. I take it that you agree?" He peered down at her in the well-lit space, and placed his hand in the small pocket of his brown vest. Arching a singular eyebrow at Margaret, Ace studied the girl's face as her cheeks flushed a slight pink in return.

"I do indeed. That is why my father and I are down here. We wished to give the McKnees some privacy to discuss an important matter without us being present." Margaret glanced over at her father, wondering if he was going to speak, or leave her to do all of the talking.

"Are you also staying at this hotel?" Thomas casually

made his way toward the couch once more, watching the sun slowly sink in the sky.

"Ah, no. I actually rent a room from a local family." Mr. Highsmith held onto his hat with his fingers, and picked at a fixed hem on the bottom of the band. His skin was tanned from working outside most of his life, and his dark brown hair was cut at the base of his neck. He was a slimmer man with a strong build, reminding Margaret of a ranch hand she knew back home. "Do you happen to know what the McKnees were discussing when you left?"

"Even if we did, why would we tell you?" Thomas asked.

"Because the sheriff instructed me to watch over you two in the event that the robbers deem you a threat. The less murders in this town, the better off for all of us." Ace comfortably maneuvered himself around the crowded décor, and found a vacant high-backed chair that was devoid of wear marks. He took a pause to adjust the belt along his waist, and sat in a manner where his gun would not damage the armrests.

Mr. Everton's brows furrowed. "A threat to whom? He has clearly shown no real sense of urgency at hearing what we have to say."

"He has a valid reason for being skeptical of your testimonies, due to your close friendship with the main suspect."

"Martin? Oh, we all know that theory is as sound as a landslip." Thomas countered. "He now believes that Mr. McKnee orchestrated the robbery from inside the hotel? He was here when it happened, and was outside in the square at the time that Adler was killed."

Ace let out a heavy sigh as he choose his next few words carefully. "Look…Mr. Everton is it? There are many facts to this case that you do not know, and I think it would be in your best interests if you leave the investigation to be handled by the ones wearing the badges."

Margaret's eyes squinted at the man, curious to see whether he truly came from the area or grew up in a neighboring county. "How long have you been renting a room from the Adlers?"

Ace's stare instantly froze, uncertain what to think about the girl sitting oddly alone in the corner. "How did you figure that out?"

"The way you touched the brim of your hat when you responded to my father's question. You focused on a stitch that had fixed a small hole near the original line, so I can presume that it was his wife who sewed it. Also, the sheriff ordered for all guests to remain in their rooms, and no one was to enter or leave the building without his knowledge. Given that you were admitted, it could either mean that you are working for the sheriff, or you knew Mr. Adler personally." Margaret decided to remain mum about their eavesdropping, but the rest were true observations she did notice.

"Very perceptive of you, I must say." Ace moved forward in the rather stiff chair. "I have been living there for a year now. I stay in the loft of the barn, in exchange for some help around the property."

"I imagine that you would like to find his killer then?"

"That would be my job, Miss." The sheriff walked into the room as though he owned the deed to the land, and cast Ace a glaring look of disapproval. "A job that can become quite dangerous for those who stand in my way."

Thomas did not care for the threatening tones coming from the sheriff's mouth. "What exactly does that mean?"

"That I feel it necessary to have Mr. Highsmith stay by your side, until you leave our town; which I hope is quite soon. Once my other deputy begins his shift for the day, then he will take your statements, and you will be free to go.

If we need you for the trial, then I will make sure you make it here safe and sound myself."

"I do not believe that Mr. Wellington took part in the robbery." Margaret boldly stated. From where she unearthed the courage to speak out loud to a man of authority, she did not know. At home, her mother always taught her to keep personal thoughts silent until an adult allowed them to be voiced. *If mother were here, she would swiftly slap me for what I am doing.* Despite her internal conflict with being so direct, she still found herself charging ahead without a moment's hesitation. "You have the wrong man."

"Oh, and is that so, Miss Everton?" The sheriff remained as tall as a statue, using his imposing height to gain the intimidation he had grown accustomed to having. "Do you have any evidence to support this claim? Because contrary to whatever *perceived* notion you have of the way I treated Mr. Wellington, I do understand the way the law works to obtain a proper conviction."

"For one thing, Gerome was left behind by the robbers. If he was a part of their group, then why did they leave him to be caught? He could tell of their plans, so the most logical choice would be to shoot him dead before escaping. Also, the two men who stole the money could not have easily crossed paths with Mr. Wellington; as he is a law student in college, and the thieves were most likely poor mine workers. Where would they have met in order to draw up the plans for going after the bank? And another thing…" Margaret stopped herself short, thinking back to what her father had said about her being too trustworthy with strangers.

"Go on." The sheriff mockingly encouraged.

"He could not have killed Mr. Adler if he was inside the bank." She flatly stated, having suppressed the detail she truly wanted to say. *I will have to talk with Father about it* before saying it to anyone else.

"I must say that your mind has been going over this in great detail. But rest assured, Miss Everton, that we are looking into other suspects, such as Mr. McKnee, for instance."

"Martin came from the hotel when the bank was robbed." Thomas defended. "Are you suggesting that he paid off these men to do the job while he was somewhere else? Because no one can be in two places at the same time."

The sheriff shook his head. "I knew you were going to vouch for him with a lie! See, Ace? Was I not right?!"

"What are you talking about?!" Thomas could feel his blood turning boiling mad. "He came up from the hotel in search of his wife and my daughter, as soon as the blast happened."

"Mr. Everton, I happened to be standing outside the front of this hotel when Wilfred came looking for me from the bank. As promised to Mr. Wise, I was ensuring that his wife and son made it to the train for their trip back to Lancaster, and had not heard the explosion from being so far away. Martin was not at the hotel at the time, because I needed to speak with him on a business matter, concerning the bank. Gene had no idea where he had gone, and a few men at the bar told me he left as soon as his wife did for the ascension." The sheriff seemed to take much joy at seeing the blank looks of confusion painted on both of the Everton's faces. "Now, if you will excuse me, I must conduct my questions of the guests before they become hostile from being confined to their rooms."

Margaret watched the sheriff head for the staircase at the same time Mrs. McKnee flew down the steps. Without acknowledging the sheriff walking by her, Kathleen managed to keep her composure together, until she reached the threshold to the parlor room. Her eyes were tinged red with sadness, and her whole face was on the verge of crying. "Can we talk?" She caught sight of Mr. Highsmith out of her peripheral. "In private?"

CHAPTER 10

Ace stepped out of the room, and closed the door while Mrs. McKnee took a moment to steady her nerves. Kathleen first wanted to apologize for the way she dismissed Thomas and Margaret into the hallway; having felt as though she abandoned them earlier. "It must have seem rather rude, and ill-mannered, of what I did. But I assure you that it was necessary if I were to…"

Thomas stopped her right there. "We did not think that for a second."

Margaret smiled in agreement with her father, wanting to display her support for the woman who had been so kind to her on their visit. "Do not fret. We harbor no anger towards you."

Kathleen gave them both a grin of gratitude on her face. "That certainly is a relief. Thank you." Her nose sniffled a touch, before she took a deep breath, and began to tell them what she learned from her husband. "Martin's first business was in selling chairs handcrafted by some friends he knew from his youth. He would go traveling around from town to town, trying to interest them in a different style…that was not well received. As time wore on, his temper was growing shorter with the people who laughed in his face. Then, in one place near Wellsboro, a shop owner's comments broke the last of his patience. After it was dark, and the man left for the saloon, Martin checked that no one was in the building. He gathered enough dry brush and twigs to help start a fire that burned the structure down to ashes. The following morning, he learned that the owner's body had been unearthed in the ruins, and fled town to avoid being arrested. There has been a warrant out for him ever since, apparently."

"Where did he go?" Margaret inquired.

"He ventured into New York for a time, and then moved into Delaware before arriving back into Pennsylvania." Her nerves were becoming rattled once more as she prepared herself for what she about to say. "And that is when he told me…that…that…his name used to be Jerome Garrison."

Jerry! Margaret shot a glance at her father that was filled with a mixture of worry and sorrow for the woman. *This is not good.*

"I realize that it looks bad for Martin, especially with all of this that I honestly never…I mean…*never* suspected of him. But I *swear* when he told me about the man's body they discovered in the ashes, he *promised* me on his mother's grave that there was no one in the house when he set that fire in motion. He even watched it go up in flames from a nearby location so no one got hurt, and is *adamant* that he had nothing to do with it." Kathleen looked pleadingly at Mr. Everton for help. "Thomas, I know that your father was a lawman, and I remember you wanted to follow in his footsteps at one time."

"Disgraced lawman, in case you forgot." He showed his discomfort in the subject, having wished to keep Margaret from ever learning about his father's poor choices in life.

"I have not. But I am asking you for your help in this matter. If Martin is arrested, I fear that the company will not recover from it." Her head lowered to watch the ground in shame. "His past will certainly destroy the well-earned reputation he has been working toward for so long. In short, we will be financially ruined." Kathleen was close to tears as she continued to speak. "It gives me no sense of pride in telling you about our money shortages. We do our best to cover it up for the mere sake of appearances, but it is worse than I had anticipated."

"Then, for the time being, we need to keep that information away from the sheriff as much as possible. Your financial status alone gives Martin a motive for going after both places." Thomas answered, purposefully ignoring his daughter's wide-eyed stare. *I guess both of our pasts have returned to haunt us.*

Kathleen's face was already starting to lighten up with a new-found hope after hearing what he had to say. "Thank you, Thomas. Please, ask me anything. I want to do my part."

Margaret could not believe her ears. Her grandfather's name was never spoken in their house, except for one night when her parents told her he was killed whilst traveling westward. To actually learn that he had been an officer of the law, disgraced by unknown factors, was as shocking as seeing a goose raising a duck as her own. She had occasionally wondered what his job had been, and imagined it differently each time; a farm hand, a newspaper man, a captain of a steamboat on the river, or maybe a soldier in the army. Each fantastical story came with a tale of sacrifice that she dreamt as a noble ending to a long-endured life. But that was evidently not the reality of it.

"So, what do we do first?" Kathleen asked Thomas, sensing the consuming tension in the air.

“We need to talk to the accused, Mr. Wellington.”

CHAPTER 11

After the sheriff denied their request to speak with his prisoner, Thomas reported the bad news to Margaret and Kathleen without surprise. "He is simply not going to allow us to speak with Gerome."

"Perhaps one of the professors at the college can help?" Kathleen suggested. "I remember Mr. Wellington saying that…" She stopped upon hearing Mr. Highsmith clear his throat, having reentered the parlor room to join in on their conversation.

"I wonder if I might be of assistance." He shyly stepped forward with a sincere look on his face, adding to the seriousness of his offer. "You were right, Miss Everton. I do want to find Adler's killer; though not to earn points with the public for the sheriff's election, as some might speculate. But as a way of repaying his kindness. Mr. Adler gave me a place to live when I was at my lowest, which is why I wish to help."

"What about leaving the investigation to the ones with badges?" Mr. Everton inquired, wondering if Mr. Highsmith was telling the truth.

"Well, since you are not going to stop looking into the

case, I might as well join in. That is, if you three will let me." He tipped his head to the right side, observing the skepticism that was still painted on their faces. "I even have a way of sneaking into the prison without the sheriff having to find out."

The trio stared at one another, silently determining whether or not to trust him. Although they each had their own reservations, given his connection to the sheriff and all, what other alternative did they really have? Nodding to one another in agreement, Thomas was the first to speak. "What is the plan?"

Ace gave them a mischievous grin. "Does anyone have a key to the bar?"

CHAPTER 12

As soon as the sheriff left for the Adler's place, Frederick helped them acquire a bottle of liquor so the group could leave the hotel and race along the sidewalks down High Street. Ace took the lead, watching for traffic crossing through the centre square, and taking them past the market-house on their right. He kept his eyes open as they neared the reverend's residence, and motioned for them to follow him to the other side of the road. "The sheriff will want to question Mrs. Adler after telling her the bad news, which should provide us with enough time before he comes back to town."

For them, maybe. But for me? Thomas kept his eye on the sun lowering itself in the western part of the sky. According to the clock on the court-house tower, the time was reaching half past five, and he still had to get home to tell Nancy they would probably be staying longer in town. *Not to mention that I could use another person on my side.* Since Coon had once worked for the stagecoaches, and seen more action than many soldiers of the day had, Thomas wanted to bring his friend back to Carlisle in case the situation got worse.

"What about the other deputy coming on duty?" Margaret asked.

"Joe does not start until six o'clock, and finishes at ten, when the civilian Night Watch takes over. He is only part-time help on the weekends…when the saloons tend to get rowdy with drunks."

Ace stopped them near the entrance to the jail, peering around to see if anyone else was watching. "Alright, you all wait here until I give the signal." He disappeared behind the door, to talk with the guard, taking the bottle of liquor in his right hand. Margaret tugged on her father's sleeve, wishing to use this opportunity to ask him a question that had been festering in her mind. But just as she was about to speak, Ace told them to come inside and escorted them down the hall.

"Gerome, you have a visitor." He announced, with an echo that sounded like a large cavern.

"Good. I was wondering when you would…" Gerome blinked his eyes twice to see if he recognized the young girl and her father, who were standing on the other side of the bars. "Do I know you?"

"I rather doubt it." Thomas gave the introductions, as Kathleen brought up the end of the line.

"Did Martin get a lawyer for me yet? I do not wish to be a bother to him if he did not." Mr. Wellington asked her.

"Actually, that is part of the reason we are here. It has to do with Martin." The group relayed what had happened in the hotel, the murder of Mr. Adler, and the sheriff trying to build a case against Martin. All the while, remaining quiet on the matter of Mr. McKnee's sorted past.

The blonde-haired law student quickly jumped further back into his cell, and away from the forbearers of doom. "Whoa. I swear I had nothing to do with any of this! That is the honest truth."

"And we believe you. That is why we are here to ask a couple of questions in the hopes of finding out who really *is* behind all of this." Thomas glanced over at Margaret, and tipped his head for her to step forward. After his daughter explained what she saw and heard just before the explosion took place at the bank, Mr. Everton also relayed the information Mr. Guthrie had told him.

After listening to their statements, Mr. Wellington slammed the palm of his hand against the wall. "That lunkhead sheriff would not know a donkey if it bit him in the…" he quickly digressed with the women being present, "well, it's Patrick Lyon all over again. That's all I have to say."

"Who?" Thomas inquired.

"Patrick Lyon was a blacksmith living and working in Philadelphia in 1798. When yellow fever struck the city, he purchased passage to Delaware for him and his apprentice. But his apprentice got sick and died once they arrived in Lewistown. He later ran into a friend from the Quaker City, who told him of a large bank heist that had taken place at Carpenter Hall. The thieves had stolen $162,821 from the Bank of Pennsylvania, and the police suspected Patrick of being the inside partner. He traveled back to Philadelphia, in order to clear his name, and the police arrested him."

"I gather from the way you have paralleled yourself to him, that he was innocent?"

Gerome nodded. "After the real robbers had stepped forth to claim that they were responsible, and Patrick had nothing to do with the crime, the police continued to hold him in the cell. He was eventually released months later, and then he sued for what they had done to him. The result ended in a wealthy payout on his behalf, but life is not all about the money. He had to endure a lot for that boatload of cash."

"We are trying to see to it that it does not happen in this case." Kathleen explained.

Gerome gave her a smile, but was hesitant to accept help from the strong-willed strangers. "I do not wish to sound ungrateful, because I am truly thankful to have someone on my side. But how do I know that you are here to help me, and not in the hopes of using me? Is there some sort of financial reward that has been promised to you, for Martin's sake, or…" He tried to delicately state his question since the ears of Mr. Highsmith were within hearing distance.

Mrs. McKnee seemed appalled at his insinuations. "Gerome! How could you think such a thing?"

"Kathleen, I know you. But we are also talking about *murder* here. Can you honestly tell me, to my face, that you would not rather see me swing from the gallows instead of Martin? I would not blame you in the least if you did."

Stepping up to the bars, Kathleen looked him square in the eye. "Whoever is guilty should pay their dues, and no one else. No matter who is at fault."

Mr. Wellington dipped his head, conceding his stance on the issue. "Then I must humbly apologize for questioning your intent. Please understand my skepticism, however. While the sheriff treats most in town with a sense of fairness, his less-than-favorable attitude towards myself… well…let us just say that it causes me to rethink charitable gifts. You will not catch me whistling before I am out of the woods."

Instead of getting into a useless debate over the meaning of charity, Thomas went straight for the point of their visit. "Now, can you tell us your story of events?"

"It was a typical morning when I awoke in my room at the East College. I kept my usual appointment with Martin, like I always do at the Mansion Hotel on Saturdays. We discussed some legal matters pertaining to the financial market, and then I went onto the bank to talk with the manager. I have been spending some of my free time with their staff as of late, to further my education of bank practices. And that is when those two men, the robbers, walked in with me."

"Did they say anything to you?"

"Only that they had been on a long road of bad streaks, and things were finally getting better for them. I said that was great news…just before they pointed a gun in my face."

"Was it a shiny revolver?" Margaret interjected.

"Yeah, it was. Sparkled like a diamond if you ask me. The one with the gun…his coat was filled with patches… ordered the tellers to load the bags with money. When the bank manager, Mr. Arnold, refused, his partner knocked him out with a blow to the back of the head. After that, the others did as they were told, and we were held captive until the one with the gun used the dynamite from his pocket to blast that hole in the wall."

Margaret attempted to work through the problem in her mind. *Something is not right. If they had the money, why wait to leave? They could have strolled away, out the front door, and blended into the crowd. Maybe the military's presence thwarted their first plan of escape? Perhaps they held out until the mounted cavalry returned to the barracks?*

"What if I told you that the gun had mechanical issues, and was in need of repair *before* the robbery took place?" Thomas added, much to Gerome's sudden embarrassment.

"Then I would feel worse than a fool in a crooked poker game."

"Speaking of poker, is there any chance that someone in debt could be involved in either of the thefts?"

Mr. Wellington chuckled. "You must be referring to Donald Sutherby." He gestured in Mr. Highsmith's direction with his head. "Ace can tell you all you need to know about the *illustrious* Mr. Sutherby, and his group of merry men. It is no secret that his games are one-sided, and his dealings rival only the devil himself in terms of sneaky wordage. He has his fingers in more people's lives than this town cares to admit."

"That is quite enough, Gerome." Ace warned. "You owe him too."

"That I do. But my amount due is nothing in comparison to others. Huh, Ace?" Mr. Wellington's smirk could not be mistaken.

"I paid that debt months ago."

Gerome cast him a perplexed gaze, but said nothing.

"Besides, mine was a mere pittance against Gene Moore and Robert Doyle's tabs. They are into him for $150.00 each."

Margaret's eyes grew wide at hearing such a large sum. Not only had Frederick been right about his boss's gambling debt, but Sutherby had a sure reason for coming after Mr. Moore. "Do you think that one of them could have done it? Perhaps the two incidents are not connected at all, and they just happened to occur on the same day."

"Mr. Moore could have been the one robbing the hotel safe, betting on everyone attending the balloon ascension, and Mr. Adler stepped in at the wrong time." Kathleen suggested, though she was hardly convinced at her own words.

"Adler was invited to work on his day off by Gene. So if that is the case, then Gene was not the intended victim and Adler's murder was…premeditated." Ace hated to say such an awful thing aloud. Adler had done life right by the Good Book, according to all who knew him, and no mean thoughts were ever harbored against the man. Greed for money had to be the explanation, right? "Elsewise, why would he ask his bookkeeper to come in?"

"Do they happen to know when Adler died?" Gerome asked. "Because there is no possible way I can be charged with his death. When I was in the bar with Martin, I remember Adler was chatting with Ron, the bartender, and was going through the tabs from prior night. As they chatted, a man came over to talk with him…someone not from around here…and asked if he could remove an item from the safe."

"What did Adler say?" Kathleen's eyes widened with intrigue.

"He told the stranger that Gene was the only one to handle all of the guests' belongings, and refused to help."

"Did the man have a black eyepatch on?" Margaret inquired, unfortunately at the same time the jail guard signaled to them that time had run out.

"It must be six o'clock." Ace interrupted. "We have to get back to the hotel before the deputy shows up for your statements." He instructed them to follow him toward the entrance, bidding Mr. Wellington farewell, and putting an end to their conversation.

Kathleen leaned into the bars, so no one else could hear what she had to say. "Is there anything you would like for me to tell Virginia?"

Gerome's head hung lower in the air than a sulking dog. "I am certain that the gossip has already reached her by now, so you can tell her to stay away from me this time. It is best for the both of us that she maintains her distance."

"Kathleen?" Thomas called from the hallway, waiting for her to join him in returning to the front of the jail. As she left, promising to deliver his message, Margaret took her chance to get a few more answers out of the prisoner.

"Why did the robbers hold you for over two hours after they got the money?"

Mr. Wellington shrugged his shoulders. "No idea. They kept mumbling to one another about someone taking too much time…though they were always too far away for me to hear who it was exactly."

"Margaret?"

Glancing over at her father, she knew it was now or never if she wanted to re-ask her question from before. "Did the stranger have an eyepatch? The one you saw talking with Adler at the bar?"

"No. But his friend did."

CHAPTER 13

"Can you hitch my wagon up, please?" Thomas asked the ostler, who was walking up from the stables with another guest's horse in tow.

"Of course, Sir." The man gave the reins to a Mr. Clifford from Newville, before returning to the stables to attend to Mr. Everton's request. According to the irritated mill owner, having been delayed from going home due to the unforeseen murder, venturing out of town after sunset was not ideal. And Thomas had to agree with him.

Despite the railroads beginning to "civilize" the countryside, as some believed it would in due time, the wilderness was as wild and untamed as the days of their forefathers. Predators lurked in the shadows of the trees, and anything was possible when it was one against the elements. Thomas hated the thought of leaving his daughter behind, but his wife was sure to go looking for them come dawn's first light, if he did not tell her they were safe. Given Martin's unscrupulous past, Thomas wondered if the woods were a better place for Margaret to be. *Should I head upstairs and demand for him to tell me where he truly was at the time of the robbery? Or would he declare me deranged and speak no more? Kathleen's judgement of character is usually sound, like her mother's was...and just because he had made a mistake long ago, does not mean he is a bad person.*

As the hotel was alive once again, with many of the guests attending the eating room, or making arrangements for transportation at the earliest convenience, the world appeared to have left the day's events behind in the dust. *To think...that somewhere...Mrs. Adler and her two children's lives have been changed forever, and yet...*

"Father?" Margaret stepped down upon the sidewalk to find her father staring blankly into the coming night. "Are you still steadfast on leaving for home this evening?"

"You know your mother, Teacher." He gave her a comforting smile after calling her by her nickname. "She would have the entire army searching for us tomorrow if she could."

"I suppose." Margaret tried to keep a brave face, but the doubts plaguing her mind were not easily silenced. "What should I do, if something does happen whilst you are away?"

Mr. Everton knelt beside his daughter, and took her hands into his, before lovingly brushing a strand of hair from her forehead. "Be strong and have faith. I will return before you can finish reading a book, have no fear of that. Kathleen will be with you, and Mr. Highsmith is to stand guard outside the door. Make sure you say your prayers, alright?"

The left corner of Margaret's mouth turned up in a partial grin. "I always do."

"And *promise* me that you will not do anything foolish until I am back tomorrow morning."

"I promise." Margaret gave her father a final hug as Kathleen called for her from inside the hotel. Hiding a tear that was ready to fall at any given moment, Margaret hurried to rejoin the others for dinner without a single glance back over her shoulders. Thomas watched on with a sense of helplessness he had not felt in years, and tossed a coin into the air with his fingers as his thoughts wandered.

"She's in safe hands." Ace's voice startled him, causing the coin to hit the ground with a metallic clink against the sidewalk.

"I am counting on it." Mr. Everton looked around the man to find his wagon being brought up by the ostler and his son. "You can shoot that gun, right?" He pointed at the holster resting on Ace's right hip.

Mr. Highsmith leaned against the brick wall of the hotel and folded his arms across his chest. "Better than anyone I know."

"Here you are, Sir." The ostler encouraged his son to climb down from the seat, and told him to hand over the note in his clutched palm to Thomas. "Bobby saw us coming out of the stables and said he forgot to give this to you when he was inside at the front desk."

"For me?" Thomas shared a puzzled look with Ace and carefully unfolded the paper that had foreboding words written on it; *Watch Your Back*. His mouth instantly went dry as he read over the nervously scribbled letters, and a knot formed in the pit of his stomach. The darkening land-scape outside of town was the perfect place for an ambush, and having Margaret with him would be a risk he refused to take. Then again, this new message made the prospect of her staying in town not much more of a comforting thought either. *What am I to do?*

Mr. Highsmith peered down at the note, whistling a section to the tune of *Old Arm Chair* as he observed Thomas creasing the paper closed. "You sure you want to head home? Sounds as though those woods might be unfriendly tonight."

"Far better for me to leave alone, than to bring Margaret with me." Thomas bent over to save his coin from the chilling ground, wishing now more than ever that Coon was already there with him. He then handed the warning note to Ace and asked him to pass it along to the sheriff in his absence. "It may not make a difference, but at least it confirms his suspicion that our lives are in danger."

"Will do." As Ace went to stuff the folded paper into his tight vest pocket, a crumpled ball of notes fell onto the ground. Thomas had barely enough time to read the letters "I.O.U." stamped at the top of the outer paper, before the man quickly stashed them away into a pants pocket.

"Is that from when you gambled?"

Ace patted the unseen promissory notes, shifting his gaze between the ground and Margaret's father. "It reminds me of what I've done in the hopes that it keeps me straighter than a loon's leg." Suddenly, Ace coughed into his hand and locked eyes with Mr. Everton, having seemingly ridded himself of whatever had been troubling him. "Thomas, I promise you that nothing will happen to Margaret. In many ways, she has the same kind of free spirit that my sister had, God bless her soul. She was all I had left in this world after my mother died. But an illness took hold of her almost overnight, and there was nothing I could do about it." He took a step backward and glanced up at the sky growing darker with each passing minute. It was something he did not take lightly in sharing. "I just wanted you to know that."

Thomas needed no further explanation from the man standing in front of him. Instantly, he knew Ace was not merely telling him the tale of a stranger's hidden grief, but it was to prove himself worthy of his promise. No clearer message had ever been conveyed to the storekeeper in such a manner before, and he felt some weight of worry lift from his tired shoulders. "Thank you." He quietly climbed atop the wagon, placed the coin into the ostler's hand, and extended his gratitude for taking good care of Josephine and Abraham.

"T'was a pleasure, Sir. Have a safe journey home." The ostler stood beside his boy as they both waved farewell to Mr. Everton, and Mr. Highsmith disappeared into the hotel without another word.

CHAPTER 14

Margaret stared out of the McKnee's room window, attempting to still her mind by studying the calmness of the stars above. But no matter what she tried to focus her troubled thoughts onto, her brain refused to pause for an evening's rest. Right after dinner, she had seen Ace hand a piece of paper to the sheriff and told him how her father received the warning just before he left town. And since then, a small seed of worry had been steadily growing in the back of her head for the last three hours. Curled up beside her bag, with a book cradled in-between her arms, Margaret closed her eyes and imagined herself working on her flying machine at home in the barn. There, she was safely lost in her own dreams of aerial navigation whilst talking away to Coon as he sat atop a pile of straw with an apple in his mouth. It was a scene that not only provided her a few minutes of peace, but also sad inner longing for Meyer's Bend.

"Cannot sleep?" Kathleen stepped out from the bedroom, dressed in a patterned-wrapper that had been sewed by Margaret's mother as a wedding present a few years ago. Standing there like a serene statue in a graveyard, the soft glow of a freshly lit candle in her right hand barely illuminated her pretty face.

"When the solution to a puzzle eludes me, it is difficult to settle my brain." Margaret glanced at the chair sitting opposite of her and invited Mrs. McKnee to join her by the window. "The stars usually help me embrace their solitude…but not tonight." She looked up again to find the sky being slowly enveloped in a band of clouds, and let an escaped sigh fog the nearby glass pane.

Kathleen accepted her offer and glanced down at the dark streets below the sill. "Concerned for your father?"

"In particular, yes. Though, there are other things that weigh almost just as heavily."

"Like the school in Chambersburg that you will be attending in the fall?"

"I am not surprised that you know, given your frequent correspondences with my mother." Margaret thumbed the corner of her book mindlessly as she spoke, the title hidden from view. "But yes. The idea of leaving Meyer's Bend for months at a time does scare me, and I will not be able to work on my flying machine whilst I am there."

Seeing the fret on Margaret's face, Kathleen decided to take a different approach to their conversation, and pointed to the darkened book. "May I ask you what you have pressed to your chest?"

"A copy of the *Account of Charles Green's Aeronautical Expedition from London to Weilburg*." The girl's eyes sparkled at being able to talk about balloon flight, and the book that their wealthiest neighbor had given to her as a gift for her last birthday. "There were three of them, who traveled 500 miles in just eighteen hours. Can you believe it? Seeing the world like those in heaven do?"

"What an amazing thing, indeed." Kathleen placed the candle on the sill, and thought back to when she was younger; to the years when most of the girls she knew made fun of her poor sewing abilities. She remembered how it felt to be awful at the domestic chores and how encouraging Nancy had been through it all. "Margaret, your parents are trying to provide the best education they can for you, I hope you realize that. Your mind is beautiful in how it works: the creative ways you see the world, the experiments you are determined to conduct, and your hidden desire for adventure. These are not all common traits."

"I suppose. Though to me, this school feels rather like an unknown factor in the middle of a larger equation."

"And is that such a bad thing?" Kathleen leaned over and patted her consolingly on the shoulder, having an idea as to what the young girl really wanted to discuss. "Would it help if we talked about the murder and the robbery instead? Perhaps speaking your ideas aloud will allow your mind to be at ease."

Margaret liked the suggestion, and started off with some of the facts that were bothering her. "If Mr. Sutherby is the one who killed Adler, then why would he choose to collect the debt Mr. Moore owed him now? At first, I thought that the upcoming election provided the perfect opportunity for him to seek payment. But all of the debts he had accumulated would be like a gold mine if he were to be elected sheriff. He could even use those to secure votes and terrorize men like Mr. Moore, once given the power to do so."

Kathleen nodded in agreement. "Currently, there is no law against soliciting votes by bribery through free drinks. And Mr. Sutherby would be the type to extend that privilege beyond all measures."

"That is if the bank robbery and the murder are connected; which, at this point, is looking far less likely than if they were two separate incidents that occurred remarkably close to one another." Margaret took a moment to adjust how she was sitting, feeling something poking her through the skirt of her dress, when a loud commotion could be heard coming from out in the hallway. "What the…"

Pounding footsteps sounded along the creaky floorboards just before a man's voice suddenly shouted into the still night. "Let go of me! I did nothing wrong! LET ME GO!"

CHAPTER 15

Both ladies peered around the door to find Mr. Moore and Frederick restraining a man who had been occupying the room beside theirs. Despite the fact that Ace's body obscured most of the scene from where they stood, Kathleen and Margaret managed to catch a glimpse of the guest himself. His clothes were of a business owner's status, and his boots were laden with mud from the long trip he had endured on the prior day. "I did nothing wrong! I have not even heard of a man called Adler! I HAVE NO IDEA WHAT IS GOING ON!"

"Ace, what is happening?" Margaret whispered, pulling on Mr. Highsmith's sleeve to grab his attention.

"Mr. Thurber had apparently left a note with a hotel employee that he was going to leave earlier today. It was forgotten about due to…other matters…and when they came up to evict him, they discovered a bloody rock under the bed."

"WHAT?!" Margaret dashed back into the room and threw her clothes on as fast as she could. *Thurber…Thurber… was his horse the one the ostler was tending to when we arrived? And that name…Thurber…I heard my mother say it before we left Meyer's Bend.* Once back at the threshold, she stepped out beside Ace and watched them struggle to drag Mr. Thurber down to the first floor. "Where is the rock?"

"Sitting on top the bed. I imagine it was wrapped in a handkerchief to keep the blood from dripping as he came upstairs." Ace cautioned her from going inside the room until the sheriff had a chance to look around, telling her about the appearance of a bag filled with stolen items from the safe.

"That is very convenient." Margaret maintained her distance while inspecting what she could see of the room from the hallway. "Why would he have risked being caught, instead of fleeing town with his bounty?"

"Some people do not have what Thomas Paine declared to be 'common sense.'" Ace pointed to an empty whiskey bottle propped on the desk by the lit candle Frederick left behind. "Mr. Moore recognized the rock as having come from the well near the Market-House. They have been restoring its walls after a storm damaged some sections almost a month ago."

"How can you tell that it came specifically from the well?"

"All of the rocks have the letter 'T' written on its surface, identifying them as having been bought by Scott Turrow. He donated them last week, and built a pile of the rocks next to the well for when they were scheduled to mend it."

Kathleen soon appeared in her proper garments, just in time to witness Margaret's face light up from making an important connection. And a wide smile shown between her cheeks as she exclaimed the good news. "It was the pirate!"

CHAPTER 16

(Somewhere on a Chicken Farm, Outside of Carlisle)

"Chance, Jerry should have been here by now." The man's sore throat was causing his voice to sound scratchier than normal. "Do you think he was caught?"

"Jerry is too good for that." Coughing into his sooty hands, the other man propped his chewed hat under his head, and draped the coat filled with patches over his tired body. "He is probably on his way right now, and taking the long way in order to avoid the posse…same as we did. There is nothing to worry about Bronco."

"But what if he was not able to find the papers? What will we do then? Huh?"

"Look, we did not locate them in the bank, so they must have been in his office."

"Are you certain they were not in his house?" Bronco chatted nervously.

"As sure as a gun's true aim. Now, would you let up and turn in for the night? We lost the posse at the creek, and doubled back enough times to confuse a seasoned wolf. There is nothing to fret over." Chance quietly played with a piece of straw protruding from his mouth, trying to drown out his own doubts on their old friend's unknown whereabouts. "Jerry knows the plan and will deliver the goods like he promised."

But his partner in crime was not convinced. "Maybe it all went wrong, and he was not able to find them. We did not leave the bank when we were supposed to. Maybe…"

"Well, it ain't my fault that the military decided not to fire the blanks from their cannons as part of the celebration, as they were supposed to! It is not as though I had a say in the matter. And we both agreed that they would have shot us dead within fifty feet if we had set off the dynamite at the time originally planned."

"We should not have entered that poker game, Chance. Jerry only wanted to help us find new work when we came here."

"I know."

"He went through so much to leave the past behind him, and we did nothing more than to drag him back into it all."

"If that were so, then why did he come to this town? He still has it out for him, mark my words."

"But Jerry's going to be awfully upset with us that we stole so much money from the townspeople. We were to take only what we owed and not a penny…"

"WILL YOU SHUT UP ALREADY?!" The man's patience was nearly gone. "Our debt is settled now, alright?" He waited for Bronco to acknowledge with a silent nod of his head. "Everything is going to work out. Sutherby is nothing anymore. He learned the hard way not to mess with us, and Jerry's to handle the rest. It does not matter what all he has done to obtain a different life…he was born a mountain man, and he will always be one of us. Come first light, we can move onto Delaware or Maryland, and then head south toward Florida to start a new life there." Settling back down in the straw of the barn, Chance closed his eyes and began to dream of what he would do with his share of the money. *No more scraping by on small earnings from tenant farming; moving around every year because the land owners say so. No more intense labor with mere coins to show for it. For now on...*

Suddenly, Chance's ears picked up on the sound of a snapping twig near the border with the woods, on the eastern most corner of the property. He calmly instructed his partner not to do anything rash as they slowly reached for their weapons. Since his gun had not yet been fixed, a fact he refused to tell Bronco, Chance knew that their escape was slim if the posse ever found their location. Especially when this countryside was unlike the mountainous terrain they learned as kids in the northern part of the state. This was mostly cultivated farmland that was shrouded in mostly pitch black darkness from a lack of moonlight. If they ran now, they would be directionally lost and at a disadvantage with the locals on their tracks. *Then again, maybe it is not the posse after all?*

"Jerry?" Chance whispered into the night. "Is that you?"

BANG!
BANG! BANG!
BANG!

CHAPTER 17

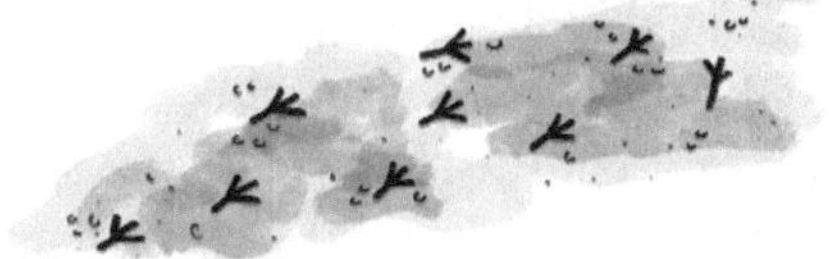

(Inside the Mansion Hotel, Carlisle)

Kathleen was the first to speak. "I am confused. How does a pirate fit into this?"

"When we were at the balloon ascension, there was a little girl beside me named Rebecca. She told me that she saw a man wearing a black eyepatch and walking away from the Market-House with a limp in his gait. But when I saw the 'pirate' later, as she called him, his limp was gone and he was searching for another person in the crowd. He was also the same man I saw in the bar before we left for the town square. And Mr. Wellington confirmed that he was a friend of the stranger who asked Mr. Adler for access to the hotel's safe."

"So this 'pirate,' stole a rock from the town's well, stashed it under his coat, and brought it to the hotel so he could kill Adler?" Ace theorized aloud.

"If Mr. Moore arranged it to happen that way. However…" Margaret tossed a few ideas around in her mind. "Mr. Adler still might not have been the intended victim."

"Because Mr. Moore asked him to come in on a day he normally had off. We all know that." Kathleen answered. "So it really could be because of gambling debts owed to

Mr. Sutherby."

Ace quickly shook his head in disagreement. "If you are thinking that Sutherby hired someone else to take care of Gene Moore, I find that difficult to believe. He prefers to handle matters himself, or to have one of his friends discreetly do his dirty jobs. Outsiders would not be trusted with something as delicate as a murder." He scratched his chin and turned his gaze upon hearing the sound of footsteps at the other end of the hall.

"Then I guess we have to ask Mr. Thurber some questions." Margaret led the charge down the stairs to find the man bound to a chair in the hotel office. The trio slowly approached the partially opened door, and listened to Mr. Moore's trying his hand at interrogating the angry guest.

"Alright, Charles Thurber. Why did you do it, huh? Did Sutherby hire you to settle my debt? It would be a trick I was not expecting from someone so firmly stuck in his ways."

"How many times do I have to you?! I have no clue as to what you are talking about, nor as to what is going on. All I remember is having a drink in the bar and gaining a massive headache afterwards. I went to my room to sleep if off, and awoke to find you searching under the bed, claiming that I killed someone; which I would certainly not do with a rock, of all things."

"That is a likely story. Since the election is soon upon us, Sutherby thought a stranger's face would go unnoticed. Admit it! He paid you to murder me because I refuse to vote for him. But instead of killing me, you accidently murdered Adler and then stole the items from the safe to make it seem as though it was a robbery that went south."

The guest's face appeared genuinely shocked to hear of the earlier theft, and began to berate the hotel manager with questions regarding the whereabouts of his box. But Gene

Moore simply smirked at the man he had tied up. "Your poor portrayal of being innocent does not fool me. We have the evidence to convict you, and that is all we need, Mr. THURBER! If that is even your real identity."

Mr. Thurber's irritation was beginning to intensify. "My name is Charles Thurber, and I am here on a business matter with Mr. James Guthrie. I know no such person called Sutherby, have no connection with whatever happened to Mr. Adler, and am quite confident that I did not steal anything from the safe."

"Well, we will find out soon enough. I have sent Frederick to fetch my brother-in-law, the sheriff, and he will be able to pull the truth out of you!"

"I would hold off on passing judgement yet." Ace flatly stated as he stepped into the room with Margaret and Kathleen flanking him on either side. "Miss Everton has a few questions of her own to ask of Mr. Thurber." He waved her into the room and invited her to do just that.

She gulped down her nerves, and stared at the business man's face, finally remembering why she had heard his name before. *Coon...Guthrie...Guns!* "If I am not mistaken, this man, named Charles Thurber, is part of a partnership that owns a gun manufacturing company in Massachusetts." Margaret paused to give the guest a chance to correct her if she was wrong.

"Yes! Someone who recognizes what I do!" Mr. Thurber released a sigh into the air. "However, we are thinking of moving to Connecticut later in the year."

Gene Moore crossed his arms to match the scowl on his face. "What has that got to do with anything?"

"Everything."

Charles Thurber hastily nodded. "The young girl is right. That is exactly my point. If I own a place that makes pistols, rifles, and guns, then why would I kill someone with a rock? I would sooner shoot the person then commit such a barbaric crime."

"But it also means that you deal in the world of inventions and patents." Margaret pivoted around on the heels of her shoes, hearing the cogs in her brain click into place. "Mr. Thurber, what was in your box that was in the hotel's safe?"

"Papers. Very important papers that contain notes and design sketches pertaining to two of my own inventions."

"Ace, run upstairs and check to see if there are any papers in the bag with the rest of the items." Gene asked in a hostile tone of voice. "We will see if that part of his story is correct."

As Mr. Highsmith reluctantly left the crowded office, Margaret thought back to what Reverend Thorn had said when she first met him in the square. "Were you recently in Philadelphia by chance?"

Mr. Thurber was surprised at what all she knew. "Just this past week. I had visited there to meet with investors in the hopes that one of them would see value in either of my inventions." The man tried to focus on Miss Everton standing off to the side in the dimly lit space, blinking his eyes as though there was a fly in the way. "Who are you, and how do you know so much about me?"

"Earlier today, Reverend Thorn told me that Mr. Wise recognized an inventor he saw whilst trying to obtain interest in his vision for Cross-Atlantic balloon travel. But it was not until a few moments ago, that I pieced together your name from what you said and a friend's recent order of a gun from your company. He happens to be a loyal customer of yours, in point of fact. I also have another friend who owns a few businesses in the city, and he sometimes discusses the latest inventions that come across his desk with me." Margaret took an important step forward, feeling free of any remaining nerves she had. "He once told me that some of his associates where 'lickspittles' at their best, and I imagine that given the right invention, they would not be above sending some hired help in order to obtain it."

"You think that Adler's death was from an attempt to steal drawings of an invention?" Mr. Moore surmised, doubt tinged his words. "Can you prove it?"

"I can." Ace raced into the office with a serious expression painted on his face. "There are no papers in the bag. Whoever is after your inventions has already taken them."

"What?!" Mr. Thurber shouted in agony. "They are probably halfway to Philadelphia by now."

Margaret tapped her index finger against her chin. "Possibly. But maybe not. To find out, we will have to talk with the farmer who sells chickens at the Market-House."

Ace nearly jumped in excitement. "There is a rooster in the stables that someone purchased earlier in the day. I saw it as I was checking around for anything suspicious while you retired to your room."

Mr. Moore asked Kathleen to stay with Mr. Thurber until the sheriff arrived, lit another candle he retrieved from a drawer, and escorted both Ace and Margaret toward the stables just down the street. As soon as he pulled the door back, Ace pointed to where the rooster was sitting in his cage. Margaret held the light up to the unhappy bird and calmly spoke to him as she stroked a few feathers. At home, she had dealt with her fair share of temperamental chickens, and used the same technique she perfected on an old hen named Molly.

Having successfully removed the rooster from his cage, she searched the straw until her hands felt the thicker material of paper crinkled underneath. Smiling from ear to ear, she grabbed the plans for Mr. Thurber's inventions out from amongst the bird's excretions, and held them up for the others to see. "I believe we have found our motive." *And that is why he choose a chicken over a pig, which would have eaten the pages.*

Suddenly, a bullet rang out from behind them, and the candle was snuffed out on its way to the ground. Ace pulled Margaret toward the back of the barn while Mr. Moore used a stack of hay bales for coverage. The rooster flapped his wings from all of the commotion, and ran screaming as he fled down the alley. Grabbing the revolver from his holster, Ace loaded the chambers before peering over the crate of supplies currently protecting them. Margaret held tightly onto the papers, determined not to allow the two men from the bar to get their greedy hands on Mr. Thurber's work. *If they get these designs, then there is nothing stopping them from leaving town and getting away with murder. Then again, what has been preventing them from going back to Philadelphia already? Maybe they stayed to ensure that Mr. Thurber was charged as the killer. Because if he is allowed to talk and fight for his designs after they had been stolen, then...*

"Look out!" Ace wrapped a protective arm overtop the girl as bullets flew through the air. With no lights along the street, no visibility inside the stables, and no moonlight to guide their vision, the suffocating darkness seemed relentless. Trying to think up a plan of attack, Ace's eyes swept around in a futile attempt to see something. *What are we going to do?*

"Ace," Margaret whispered, "look." Although her hand was still cloaked in the void of night, he could sense where she was pointing. Coming through a small window in the far corner, a stream of moonlight shined directly upon a door latch near the back wall.

Mr. Highsmith lowered his voice so she would be the only one to hear what he was going to say, and spoke plainly so there would be no misunderstanding his words. "Margaret, listen very carefully to me. I am going to cover you until you reach the door, and escape with those plans."

"Then what do I do?" She kept her voice as steady as possible.

"Run. Run toward Reverend Thorn's house if you can, across the street from the jail. Promise me that you will do that."

"Yes, Sir. I promise." Margaret could feel her fear bubbling inside her stomach as she started over for the door, waiting for the sound of gunshots to pierce the air once again. After Ace fired a round or two, she rushed to the latch and threw open the door to find the street barren while the shots continued inside the barn. By now, a few voices could be heard from the neighboring houses as people were beginning to stir from the gunfire being exchanged by both sides.

Staring her down was a darkened labyrinth of streets spread out before her in *all* directions. Faintly illuminated by the moon, that was managing to penetrate through the clouds above, Margaret instantly felt isolated in the foreboding place. What scared her even more than the darkness itself was the hidden danger lurking where she could not see.

Gathering her bearings, she marched easterly on Church Alley, before heading northward to rejoin onto High Street, just past the court-house. Coming up to the centre square, Margaret was about to cross the street, when her heartbeat stopped at the pounding of running feet she could hear closing in from behind. Panic drowned out all reason in her mind as she raced toward the market-house, only to find a drunken man sitting on the sidewalk. He reached for her, speaking loud enough to raise the dead and with ill-mannered words that were difficult to deduce in his slurred speech. Just as the moonlight faced from view once again, she managed to escape and sprinted to the northern side of High Street.

Racing up Hanover, Margaret passed by the bank in a matter of seconds. She wondered where all of the Night Watch had gone, since Mr. Sutherby had suggested they double their numbers that evening. *I sure hope that drunk man is not all there is tonight.* Still, the sound of pounding feet were relentlessly pursuing her further up the brick-paved walk, leading her farther away from the jail and Reverend Thorn's house. As the moon's beams returned on the other side of a thin cloud, Margaret squinted to her left to find the shadow of a person she hoped would be an ally.

She nearly tripped on the curb as her chest was starting to labor and her blood was pumping pure adrenaline to stay alive. Faster and faster she demanded her legs to carry her toward the corner of Louther Street, where an old grocery and provision business stood; all the while she listened to the man with the eyepatch shouting at her to stop. "GIVE ME THE PAPERS AND NO ONE GETS HURT! GIVE THEM TO ME!"

From the west side of Louther, Ace Highsmith had finally caught up to the chase, having seen Margaret head north instead of east off the square. His eyes widened in fear when he saw where she was going, and he raced to warn her of the neglected well she was heading straight toward. He wasted no time in rushing to her aid, forgoing the idea of calling out to her and possibly making the situation even worse.

Resisting the urge to turn around to see if the man was gaining on her, Margaret continued on until she reached the shadow and felt the wind being stolen from her lungs. It was not being casted by a person who might help her, but instead from a saddle drying outside the landowner's building. Despite wanting to cry in despair on the inside, Margaret tried looking for a potential weapon nearby that she could use to defend herself. *What to do, what to do!*

"AH-HAH! I have you cornered now!" The man with the eyepatch spatted out. A chunk of saliva escaped his mouth whilst he lunged for the papers in her hand. "Give them to ME!"

Margaret turned to face him, stepping back out of reach and closer to the haphazardly-covered well. Her foot soon stepped on a weakened ledge of the wooded planks where the loose rocks of the remaining wall were still crumbling. She instantly froze out of fear; unsure where to move with the light being so poor where she stood. Unable to blink, her heart was playing louder than a drumline in her ears. All of a sudden, the man's fingers latched onto the papers and he tried to rip them from her grip.

"NO YOU DON'T!" Ace launched himself at the man with the eyepatch, allowing Margaret to take a leap of faith in the direction she believed to be solid ground. For a moment, the two men struggled and fought in the darkness without being able to see the tips of their own noses. Margaret held her breath for the moon to break through the cloud coverage once more, putting a small beam of light directly on the property.

Ace could tell that the other man was stronger, and he was bound to overpower him very soon. Nevertheless, he swiftly released his grasp on the man's wrist long enough to punch him in the face right before his neck was being constricted by the killer's hands. It was now or never if Ace wanted to get out from under the other man's hold. As his right foot slipped on a loose rock from the edge of the well, an idea popped into his mind. Using all of the force he had left, Ace ducked downward, removed his grip on the other man's arms, and caught him off-balanced.

The man with the eye patch yelled into the night as he fatally plunged head first into the deep and cavernous well. But just when Ace thought he was clear of the steep ledge, the man's boot nicked Ace's shin and he suddenly felt gravity pulling him toward the gloomy depths below. His arms flew into action, grabbing ahold of the walls with the type of strength only mustered by the will to stay alive. Watching in dread as his crumpled promissory notes fell from his pocket, Ace focused on his breathing to steady his mind and tried not to think of the long fall under his stomach.

Margaret ventured as close as she dared, and looked on helplessly from the side, not wishing to accidentally push him into the water. She asked him if there was anything she could do to assist him, but Ace simply told her to stay where she was.

Using every muscle in his body, Ace slowly and cautiously inched his way over to solid ground. He waited until he could feel the grass underneath his knees to make a final lunge for safety, and let out a sigh of relief as his head landed on the cool soil. With his lungs heaving from his near death experience, Ace had never been more grateful to still be living than he was in that moment. The grass was crisp to the touch, the sky ever so beautiful, and the night air was that much sweeter to his senses.

Margaret rushed up to hug him, thanking him profusely for saving her life. She proudly showed him the papers clenched in the palm of her hand and asked if they could return to the hotel. "The sheriff should be there by now, and these will be much safer in his care."

Ace could not help but smile at the little girl whose eyes were twinkling at him. There was no denying the resemblance she shared with his beloved sister, and he was instantly taken back to his ten-year-old self. The way her face would light up a room, and her calming presence that made everything seem alright, were both traits he sorely missed since her passing. Staring at Margaret, all of the good memories from his childhood flooded his mind and pulled him even deeper into the fold. "It would be my pleasure. The sooner those pages get locked up, the better it will be for all of us."

CHAPTER 18

"What do you mean the sheriff will not be here for another few hours?!" Ace was starting to lose his temper with the hotel worker standing behind the counter. From what happened at the barn, Margaret was right that the man with the black eyepatch had not been alone. And the idea of a potentially vengeful friend did not sit well in the back of his mind.

"Just what I said, Sir. I went to the sheriff's house under Mr. Moore's instructions, and was told that he had already been called out east of town. She said the posse located the bank robbers on Duncan's chicken farm." Frederick explained.

Mr. Highsmith's eyes widened at the surprising news, and his heartbeat raced a little faster. "Do you know if they arrested them or if there was a shoot-out?"

"The sheriff's wife said nothing on that matter, Sir."

As Ace tried to find out more information from the man who had no answers for him, Margaret shyly stepped up to Mr. Thurber inside the hotel manager's office. She wondered what his inventions were truly about, and studied his drawings from looking over his shoulder. The business owner had been giving them a thorough checking to see if any of his notes were missing or torn from the pages. Apparently satisfied that everything was in order, Charles Thurber's face broke into a smile and he rested easier in the chair. "All is well. Thank heavens."

"If I may, what do your inventions do?" Margaret asked.

He pushed the top paper closer to her on the desk and described what he called a "typewriter for the nervous and the blind." It was a machine with a large wheel that had metal rods arranged around the outer rim. Atop the horizontal keys were letters one could feel through their fingertips, and a roll of paper that would be stamped with the same letter after pressing the key downward. While the object's scale might have presented a production problem, the overall concept was quite intriguing in Margaret's opinion. "But I also have the idea for something called a 'Mechanical Chirograph' that I have been developing in the study of penmanship and…" Mr. Thurber abruptly stopped upon hearing the door to the hotel fly open, and a man dressed in night attire began shouting for help.

"The barn is on fire! Mr. Moore is trying to save the horses!"

Ace and Frederick ran outside to assist Gene in getting the animals to safety, leaving the others alone in the office. Margaret had a sinking suspicion that the fire was no accident, and she shared a worried glance between Mr. Thurber and Kathleen. "He is still out there, you know. The man who was with him."

"Perhaps we should go upstairs to our hotel room and wait for Ace to return." Mrs. McKnee suggested, to which Mr. Thurber nodded in agreement.

"Being higher up, we will be able to see anyone coming or going."

Margaret also thought it was a good idea, and hastily picked up a group of blank papers from the desk to curl up like the original drawings. *Having a duplicate set might come in handy at some point.* "Ready to go?" She walked toward the office door while the other two collected the real plans from their scattered state on the desk. All seemed quiet in the deserted lobby as she swept her gaze around the area and listened for any signs of movement. But as she stepped past the threshold, the door was slammed shut behind her. Looking up to her immediate left, her heart nearly stopped as she saw the same man who bumped into her earlier that day.

"GIVE ME THE PAPERS!"

Margaret ran for the stairs as the man locked Kathleen and Mr. Thurber inside the office with Adler's key. She rushed up the steps faster than a dog after food, and didn't stop until she found herself trapped at the end of the third floor. Her skin went cold as ice when she heard his footsteps racing after her. Desperately, she pulled on the door handles to all of the rooms without any success. There was no hiding this time. *All I have is to hope that the dark hides me at the back of the hall.*

When the sounds of his feet suddenly ended at the top of the stairs, her stomach plummeted to the ground and she turned around to face the bleak void staring straight back. Margaret's ears strained to hear the faintest of movements, signifying where the man was standing. She dared not to speak and covered her mouth; for fear that her breathing was becoming too heavy. Seconds ticked by like hours, where no creaks could be heard from the floorboards, nor did his coat brush against the walls. Quietly…anxiously… nervously…Margaret stood like a statue, dreading the inevitable moment when he would find her.

As the clouds parted, the moon's light soon fell through a singular window that allowed her to see a small portion of the empty space. Margaret secretly wished that the man would move into the outlined rectangle, giving her time to jump out of the path of any oncoming bullets. But as a threatening arm rose against the moonbeam, and the man's body was still shrouded in darkness, the silhouette of a unique weapon came forth. It appeared to be a knife blade and revolver merged into a fatal duo for double the effectiveness. The top of the long Bowie knife held a hidden gun barrel capable of shooting .12 mm cartridges from a pin-fire revolver, which had already taken many lives.

Margaret braced herself, having nothing within reach to fend off his aim.

"This is for my brother!" As his finger pulled on the trigger, one of the doors to her right opened up, and an absent-minded guest poked his head out to see what was going on. The bullet became lodged in the door and Margaret leaped into the room without any hesitation.

She could feel her heart beginning to beat again while the startled guest slammed the door closed and demanded an explanation for the disruptive shooting.

"Margaret?!" Ace's voice suddenly came down the hall, alerting the killer to his presence in the hotel.

"He's in the hall, Ace!" She shouted at the top of her lungs in the hopes that he could hear her.

Two additional shots pierced the wooden door, ripping the guest's robe and causing them both to hide behind a chair for protection. That was when Margaret caught the sound of another struggle taking place in the hallway, and she peered above the armrest as though she could see through the wall. The fight continued for a few seconds more, until a different shot silenced the noise altogether. A large thud rang out as a man's body crashed to the floor in front of the room she was hiding inside.

"ACE?!" Margaret shouted. She waited to hear him respond in good spirits, but the air remained as quiet as before. Panic filled her mind as she called his name even louder. "ACE!! ACE!!"

The male guest helped her to push the door open against the weight that was holding it closed, and her heart instantly split into two. "NO!" Margaret cried as she saw his dying body lying next to the other man across the floor. Blood seeped from the matching wounds they both sustained from a single bullet, fired from the gun still smoking hot in Mr. McKnee's left hand. His face shocked to a sickened white from the realization of what he had done.

"I…I…that man turned Ace in front of the bullet after I shot. Margaret, please believe me." His mouth hung lower than a drawbridge, unable to talk without stuttering every other word. "Margaret…I…I…"

She swung her head back to Ace's limp form, and his skin that was already becoming ghostly pale under the cloak of night.

CHAPTER 19

Margaret may have been physically present at the church service the following morning, but her mind was still trying to process the tragic death of Mr. Highsmith. Although she had not slept a wink before the sun greeted the day with promise, Margaret had never felt more awake in her whole life. Each time her eyes closed, Ace's lifeless face always stared back.

Kathleen poked her in the side with an elbow, prompting her to stand as everyone began to sing from the hymnals. Margaret glanced over the words, softly saying them with minimal effort as her fingers passed over the notes with indifference. In her heart, she did have a renewed sense of gratitude for having lived through the night. However, she could not shake her thoughts away from what had transpired in the early hours of the morning.

The sheriff had arrived at the hotel moments after the fatal bullet had killed both Ace and the other man. Despite the fact that finding Mr. McKnee with the gun in his hands should have pleased him, there was no smirk on the sheriff's lips nor was there a glint in his eyes. As the blood cooled and stopped spreading, the gravedigger came for the measurements like before, and the sheriff presided over the whole thing with a stoic face. Kathleen had taken Margaret down to the parlor room so her statement could be documented once the bodies were removed from the building.

Waiting for the sheriff to ask her any questions, Margaret could not help but stare at the blank pieces of paper crushed in her hands; wondering how someone could feel the need to commit murder, all for the sake of greed. By the time the sheriff had ventured their way, the scene almost felt like a nightmare that would never end…if only she woke up.

Margaret explained to the sheriff about finding the designs in the chicken's cage, the man with the eyepatch falling into the well on Louther Street, and finally about the fight that ensued on the third floor. The sheriff did not interrupt her as she spoke, noting where and when the series of events took place on a notepad of paper. He even gave her a moment to finish her last few words, before addressing Mrs. McKnee about her husband's involvement.

Since he shot the gun to save Miss Everton, the sheriff felt that a jury would not convict him for murder, but that all of the proper procedures had to be followed anyway. A mutual understanding seemed to pass between them, along with a feeling of sadness for what happened. After all, Ace had been the sheriff's preferred choice to be his successor.

A small touch of Kathleen's hand brought Margaret back to the present, and she rose with the congregation as the service came to a close. Reverend Thorn asked Miss Everton if she was doing alright, to which her muted reply was answer enough. He wished her a safe trip homeward, and then went about seeing to the church's afternoon picnic.

One of the deputies escorted the two women to the hotel, where the Evertons had been waiting in the lobby with Coon. At the sight of her mother, Margaret instinctively ran into her arms for a warm embrace she wished would last forever. Frederick had been regaling them with what occurred in her father's absence, which gained a scolding look from her parents, and a highly impressed Coon to their left.

"What about your promise not to do anything foolish until I returned?" Thomas asked.

"Well, I did what you would have done." Margaret shyly replied.

"And I would be remiss if I did not say that I am mighty glad she did." The sheriff walked up to them from the direction of the office, tipping his hat to Mrs. Everton and Mrs. McKnee as he approached. "She pieced the puzzle together faster than a rattlesnake can bite. Though, I would not encourage such a dangerous avenue in the future. Someone might actually get to finish what they set out to do next time."

"Oh, there is no worry on that, because there will NOT *be* a next time." Mrs. Everton loudly declared.

"Tell me something Sheriff." Mr. Everton took a step forward, indicating that he was not going to shrink in the man's presence. "Did you really think that Mr. Wellington was a part of this whole sorted affair?"

"Yes and no. Gerome does have a tendency to push the boundaries in what he considers to be fun. Stealing from a bank, however, is a little too bold for him."

Margaret was starting to follow where her father was heading with his questions. "Arresting him was your way of sparing him from a potential lynching?"

The sheriff grinned, curling his mustache at both ends as he addressed Thomas. "You may think what you like of me, Mr. Everton. Although everyone has a right to their own opinions in this life, many judge without a second thought. But I do care about my job and the people of this town. What I did was not only for the good of Mr. Wellington, but also for the good of the people who were mad. There was no telling what a mob like that would have done."

"He will be released soon?" Kathleen inquired as the sheriff turned to face her.

"Tomorrow morning. I will be personally escorting him to class."

"Why did they do it?" Margaret ignored her mother's attempts to keep her quiet. "The robbers, I mean. They were not normal highwaymen, were they?"

"No, they were not. From what we have discovered, one of them was a prior coal miner and the other a farmer. Some folks had admitted to seeing them around town, but if anyone knows their names, they are not talking. All we can figure is that they were waiting for a third person in their group to join them before they left for good. Most likely the one you heard them say at the bank, Miss Everton."

Jerry. Margaret thought to herself. *Whoever Jerry is.*

CHAPTER 20

"All loaded and ready to go!" Thomas called from the front entrance of the hotel. He had the horses drinking some water from a few buckets while Coon was dangling his legs off the back end of the wagon.

Kathleen was near tears as she hugged Nancy, remembering what it was like when they were both young girls in Meyer's Bend. "This town will not feel the same after this weekend." She pulled herself away to dab her cheeks dry. "We only had a mere hour to talk, and there is so much I feel we have to catch up on."

Nancy held her friend's hands in her own, giving her a farewell smile that was more caring than sad. "We are not that far you know. And one never forgets the way back home."

"Thank you for everything." Margaret wrapped her arms around Mrs. McKnee and wished her well. "Please write to me while I am in school."

"Of course I will." Kathleen patted her shoulders and helped the young girl climb onto the wagon's high seat.

As the Evertons were about to leave, however, the ostler and his son hollered for them to stop. "Wait! Wait!"

Out of her peripheral, Margaret caught sight of the rooster in the cage that the Charles Thurber's papers had been stashed. She was grateful that all of the animals survived the fire unscathed, and that Mr. Thurber was given permission to head home, but wondered why they were chasing them down.

"Mr. Everton, Sir," the ostler slowed when he reached the family, "we have no place for this rooster. The sheriff said to return him to the farmer, but he does not want him back. Says that he was happy to get rid of the mean beast in the first place."

Thomas looked at his wife, who shrugged when he asked with his eyebrows. "Well, Margaret, what do you say?"

Her face lit up in surprise. "You think it would be alright?"

"Fine by us."

Margaret eagerly reached for the cage from the ostler's son and thanked them for trying to re-home the poor bird. She handed him over to Coon for securing in the wagon as her father started the team toward Meyer's Bend.

"Do you have an idea of what to name him?"

Looking up at her father, Margaret did not hesitate to respond. "I will call him Ace."

CHAPTER 21

(Months Later, In October - 1843...)

Margaret watched the bag floating in the air, filled with smoke from the fire she lit in the middle of some rocks. No matter how many times she had conducted that same experiment, it never grew tiresome to hear her fellow students' joy at seeing the bag defy gravity. Even though some of them had witnessed a balloon ascension before, the science behind it was still a mystery to most. "The Montgolfier brothers believed that the more foul smelling the smoke, the higher the lift would be that was generated from the gas."

"Why did they not simply use hydrogen?" An interested blonde-haired girl asked, standing near the front of the small gathering.

"Well, it was far too expensive to make at the time, a rather risky endeavor, and would escape much easier than…" Margaret suddenly stopped upon hearing the sound of a teacher's voice calling them all back to class. As the others grabbed their books, and rushed back to school, Margaret took a few moments to douse the fire with water. After being assured that the flames were no more, she packed up her supplies and hustled into the building right before the teacher closed the door shut. "Sorry, Miss

Ashford."

"At least your sense of time has vastly improved, Miss Everton." The teacher's eyes peered through rounded glasses that had seen better days. Two scratches were visually noticeable on her right lens, which almost lined up perfectly with the scar she obtained as a child. Some of the newer students speculated under their breath, what could have been the cause to such an obvious mark on her face. But Margaret already knew about the previous carriage incident from an older student, and refused to join in on the snickering at lunch. That is why she opted to wander outside instead, continuing to play with different materials in her studies of the wind. Once the others discovered what she was doing, they soon became intrigued by her knowledge, and would sometimes join her in the yard; as now, she was considered to be one of them, despite her still feeling like an outcast on most days.

"I promise to do better next time around." Margaret's face blushed a slight pink as she crumpled the bag behind her back and turned to walk down the hall.

"Wait a minute there." Miss Ashford stepped up in her noisy boots, and gingerly held out an envelope in front of the young student. "This arrived for you in the day's mail."

Margaret's eyes widened, seeing all the hall empty as the others filed into the classrooms for the beginning of class. Without truly reading the handwriting, and believing it to be a letter from her parents, Margaret hastily thanked her for delivering the envelope and hurried to the class stationed at the opposite end. She managed to slip into the room right before a stern-looking woman moved swiftly through the threshold.

"Well, I do hope that all of you will be…" The woman's voice trailed off as the classroom hushed their words. "Now that I have your attention." She coughed in the air, a way of silencing the last of the rebels with a subtle warning. "If you all would please remain in your seats, as I locate where your new Antiquities teacher is, none of you will have to stay late. But if I find even ONE student out of their chair when I return, the entire class will be in the kitchen for the next three days. Is that clear?"

Their voices rang out in unison, waiting for the woman to leave so they could talk about the latest dresses at the shop in Chambersburg. Margaret, on the other hand, had the chance to really look over the envelope she had shoved inside a book she was borrowing from another girl. Since the school supplies were sold at the equivalent prices to those purchased in Philadelphia, the Evertons were not able to afford all of the required materials. They had spent some of their calculated funds on paying for drawing and painting to be added to her curriculum, and mailed her a few coins every other week to satisfy her sweet tooth. But as she moved the envelope from the book, she thought it odd her fingers felt no bumps.

Flipping it over to the front side, she suddenly realized that the address was not done in her mother's handwriting. It was foreign to her; the way the letters swooped and dipped in the spelling of her name. Even the postmark in the corner was from a place she had never heard of before. Curiously, Margaret opened the flap to reveal a folded letter inside, that had been written by the very man she visited Carlisle to see in the spring.

Dear Margaret,

It pains me to say that this letter has waited far too long to be written. Forgive me for the length of time that has passed, since my ascension from the welcoming town of Carlisle. I did not wish to write to you, until the plan was certain and approved by your seminary.

Within three weeks, I plan to visit Chambersburg, to give a demonstration of a new balloon I finished two nights ago. After speaking with your parents, as well as Mr. and Mrs. Burns, it is my great honor to have you assist me in my future ascension, and to give you privileged knowledge in reference to a lecture they asked me to do at your school. You will find three more sheets of paper, sent along with this letter, providing the notes I wish to discuss with your fellow students. Please review my notes, as I look forward to speaking with you about such observations upon my arrival on the 20th.

My kindest regards,
John Wise

P.S. The fascinating events that transpired on May 27th, were told to me by Reverend Thorn, in a letter much like this one. He wrote to inform me as to the part my balloon played in discovering the robbery, and I found it to be quite a fantastical notion indeed; For I had not been pointing to the bank at all, but rather, to a fallen tree that had trapped a dog under its trunk.

I am pleased to say that the Reverend mentioned having seen the dog walk again, without any issues.

Margaret almost pinched herself to eliminate the possibility that she was dreaming. Here she was, sitting in the middle of a classroom in the countryside, reading a letter written to her by one almost as renowned as Charles Green, and she could not have felt more elated. *I just wish Mother and Father could see it.* She quickly re-read the message over again, feeling a twinge of bittersweet feeling for the town she could never forget, and a longing for familiar grounds. *Or Coon...I miss being home.* Slowly folding the pages back into the envelope, Margaret looked up to the front of the room just as the lady walked in with another female in tow.

"Class, please welcome the latest addition to our teaching staff, Miss Vectra Tillerman."

Everyone's faces were all different shades of curious and skeptical judgement, staring at the woman who was formally dressed, but had a wild air about her mannerism. Dark hair, thick and wavy, had been restrained into a bun nearly bursting from the seams, and the bonnet she removed from her head, was made from imported cloth not locally sold. Her plaid dress was impeccably made with a tailored finish, leaving them to wonder why a woman with such fine taste was working as a school teacher. The woman's skin was not as fair as many, though far from being considered a lower-class worker.

"Thank you for the introduction, Miss Mayflower. I am sure that the class and I will get along just fine." She blinked at the woman, with a sassy note in her eyes, and proceeded to close the door with a smile painted on her face. Turning back to the girls awaiting her instructions, and pulling a light wrap off her shoulders at the same time, Miss Tillerman did not hesitate to use the large chalkboard on the wall. "Now, can someone inform me as to where your previous teacher had you reading in the school's provided book?"

"We were just beginning our section on Greece, Miss." One of the more popular girls from the front row quickly answered, her lips drawn in a grin as she causally placed her fingers by the expensive cameo necklace she was wearing.

"Excellent." Miss Tillerman mischievously smiled at the wall, where the other could not see.

"Do you know a lot about the Greeks and Romans?" Asked a taller student from the second row near the back, clearly wondering what the rest of them were eager to know.

Their new teacher turned around to face them once again. "Oh course I know about the Greeks and Romans. Would you expect this school to hire anyone not adequately prepared for the job at hand?" With the question of her qualifications at rest, Miss Tillerman had the class open their books to page 140, and began with their lesson for the day. "Now, in order for us to fully understand the relics from a civilization long since gone, we first need to try thinking like they did. Seeing what they viewed, so we can learn from what happened. Who can tell me about Archimedes' principle on buoyancy? Miss Everton?"

Margaret brought herself back to reality from her daydreams, and saw the others all starring at her from their seats. A gulp caught in the back of her throat, as the pressure from the attention was beginning to seep in. She suddenly felt a nervous knot in the bottom of her stomach, until she saw the teacher wink at her. Her nerves eased almost immediately, and the general store didn't feel so far away. *Perhaps everything is going to be alright here.*

For she would never find out that it was Ace Highsmith's father who died all those years ago near Wellsboro, and that his middle name was "Jerry."

THE END

RESEARCH QUESTIONS

1. Is the Story of Patrick Lyon True?

Yes. When Gerome Wellington tells the others about the case of Patrick Lyon and the stolen money from the Bank of Pennsylvania, many of the details are accurate to the account that had been published by himself, on his own case. He was a blacksmith who had been placed in charge of working on the safe before he left the town with his apprentice. As he was no longer in Philadelphia at the time, he had no knowledge of what occurred until an old friend told him, and he went back to clear his name. The State awarded him with a large sum of money after he sued for wrongful imprisonment.

2. Who could be a sheriff in Pennsylvania in the 1840s?

Pretty much anyone could be a sheriff in the early 1800s. There was no test, or written rules that one had to pass in order to obtain a badge. It was a job that was highly sought after, and many different candidates would go against one another each election season. It was also not against the law to bribe voters outside the voting booth with alcohol at the time, and would cause some cases of rowdyism in the streets.

3. Who was John Wise?

John Wise was instrumental in helping to establish American's love for ballooning in the 1800s. He took countless flights, or ascensions, into the air from all over the country, and even tried convincing the government to include aeronauts in the Union Army during the Civil War (although, Thaddeus S.C. Lowe was more successful in that endeavor). But despite all that is known about his life, well-detailed in his book Through the Air from 1879, Mr. Wise disappeared over Lake Michigan on his final flight and his body was never found.

For book discussion questions, more behind-the-scenes research, and art/book-ish news, please visit my website.

Did you like this story? Be sure to spread the word and tell your friends. And don't be afraid to post a review! Thanks in advance.

ABOUT THE AUTHOR:

Sarah Ickes has her Associates Degree in Art and Design. She has always held a passion for writing since her first publication of a poem in fifth grade. Not only does she pursue writing, but she also creates artwork that is available for purchasing; such as the illustrations and book cover of this novel. History is of a special interest to her, as she enjoys learning about the past. Please visit her website for more details or follow her on social media.

www.SarahIckesArt.com

Thank you for reading my book, and I hope you enjoyed it!